"What you...
is you're...
another time, correct?"

She nodded.

"Don't you think I'd have to be a little crazy to believe you?"

"But look at me. Do I look like any of the women you know? Have you ever seen a pen like that before, or a cigarette lighter, or the calculator I showed you last night? Have you ever seen a color picture before? Have you ever heard music like I played for you?"

"I don't believe in stuff like that. Traveling back in time."

Lauren sighed. "I don't either. At least I didn't before."

"You got any other proof?"

"Quite a bit. She took out all of the money from her wallet and spread it on the table in front of him. "Look at the dates on it," she said.

He spent a long time examining the money while she reached over and took another of his cigarettes. If only he'd believe; if only he would help her.

He finally looked up from the money and said, "Why'd you have to pick on me? Of all the thousands of men in San Francisco, why me?"

BEVERLY SOMMERS

Time and Again

WORLDWIDE

TORONTO • NEW YORK • LONDON • PARIS
AMSTERDAM • STOCKHOLM • HAMBURG
ATHENS • MILAN • TOKYO • SYDNEY

TIME AND AGAIN

Worldwide Library/August 1987

ISBN 0-373-97042-0

Printed in U.S.A.

Prologue

LATER, for lack of anything else to blame, Lauren blamed McDonald's. But when all the McDonald franchises in the world instantaneously disappeared from the face of the earth, so to speak, she felt little consolation. What would she do when the next "Big Mac Attack" hit her?

Everything started out so normally. What could be more ordinary than spending Christmas with her family in Los Angeles, then making the drive back to San Francisco along Pacific Coast Highway. This time she had made a couple of stops along the way: the first one in Big Sur to spend the night with her old college roommates and exchange news; the second one in Santa Cruz to see a former boyfriend and patch up some bad feelings he still had over their breakup.

She was glad now she'd decided to stop off and see him, to celebrate New Year's Eve together. Mitch had been a little put off at first when she'd refused to share a joint with him, and he'd made fun of the more traditional bottle of champagne she had brought along. One of the major reasons for their breakup had been his heavy use of drugs, and even though he swore he only smoked an occasional joint now, Lauren didn't want to encourage him.

The evening had been fine, though. He got a little high, she got a little drunk, they talked over old times, toasted in the New Year. Mitch hadn't even given her a hard time when she insisted on crashing on his couch. When she left that morning it was with the sense that their friendship had been repaired, which gave her a good feeling: she wasn't one to leave former friendships in disarray.

There wasn't much traffic on the highway. She figured most people were at home either recovering from the night before or watching the Parade of Roses. She didn't care about the parade, but she wanted to get home in time to watch the Rose Bowl. Watching the Rose Bowl was a tradition in her family, and she had kept it up over the years.

She hadn't eaten much breakfast. Mitch had fed her some nasty-tasting cereal, some kind of health food mix, and she had barely touched it. Her stomach started to growl outside of San Francisco, and when she saw a McDonald's, she pulled off the highway and into the parking lot. She might as well eat now. It was unlikely she had anything in the refrigerator at home, and the grocery stores wouldn't be open because of the holiday.

Once out of the car she noticed that the sky was clouding up and the air was considerably cooler than when she had set off that morning. She put on her black leather jacket—a Christmas present from her parents—then, so she wouldn't have to lock the car, she grabbed her duffel bag of red rubberized nylon and slung it over her shoulder. She headed inside with nothing more momentous in mind than having a Big Mac and a large Coke.

She had never been in an empty McDonald's, and this one was no exception. A group of teenagers was sitting in one corner with a stereo cassette player as big as a small car, the sounds of Billy Idol pouring forth from its speakers. A few families with young children occupied some of the other tables. Two California highway patrolmen sat at a table by the door, and she automatically checked them out as she headed toward the counter to order. In San Francisco she checked out *any* men who looked as though they might be straight. These two resembled surfers more than cops, and she caught the eye of the one with the bushy blond mustache as she passed them.

At the counter she decided she was hungry enough for a large order of fries as well as a Big Mac. The patrolmen were just leaving as she settled down at a nearby table with her food. The blonde appeared willing to join her if she gave him any encouragement, but she didn't really see any point in it and instead pretended a greater interest in her food than was warranted.

As she was finishing her burger, the radio station announced the scores of some of the football games, and then the music started up again, an oldie by the Beach Boys this time. Glancing at her watch, she saw it was almost time for the Rose Bowl to start.

She gathered up the empty containers, shoved them into the trash bin and headed for the front door. Pulling her sunglasses down over her eyes, she reached out and pushed the door open. It was at that exact moment that she felt the earth tilt, heard the sound of glass shattering and was thrown several feet from the entrance, ending up unceremoniously in a heap in the parking lot, her duffel bag cushioning her fall.

Being a native Californian, she immediately thought *earthquake*. She could hear screams, and she saw several of the teenagers run out of the restaurant. People who had just pulled into the parking lot had got out of their cars and were racing for shelter inside. For the life of her she couldn't remember all the earthquake warnings she had heard. She knew she was supposed to take cover either inside or out but wasn't sure which. The only thing she remembered for certain was that if you were inside you were supposed to stand in a doorway.

She stood up and was coming to the conclusion that she had better go back inside McDonald's and take cover when she felt another shock, larger this time, and saw the asphalt buckle beneath her feet. In dire need of something solid to hold on to, she ran back to McDonald's and grabbed the corner of the building, gripping it tightly while she watched the world go haywire.

Shattered glass lay everywhere, and even as she held on to the stucco building for support she could see the cracks forming. The walls appeared to be crumbling within her grasp, and she heard screams close by before realizing that she was the one doing the screaming.

The quake was much stronger than she had originally supposed, stronger than any she had experienced thus far in her life. Frightened, she was about to make a dash for her car and huddle inside it for protection from the flying glass when the earth rocked again, and she looked in the direction of the parking lot just in time to see the ground open up and swallow her VW whole along with a few other cars, some with people inside. She felt her stomach turn over and could taste the Big Mac backing up into her throat. She bent double and vomited the hamburger and the fries and probably her breakfast, dropping to her knees and continuing to heave long after nothing more would come up. When at last the convulsions halted, she raised her head and scanned the area where the cars had been, but saw only broken asphalt.

The thought came to her that maybe this was the "big one," the one that was supposed to separate California from the rest of the country. Now, above the screams, she could hear sirens in every direction. Terrified, she lurched back toward the restaurant just as the earth seemed to rise up. For a split second she was standing on a small hill that hadn't been there before, then she was flying through the air. Only this time she must have landed on her head, because suddenly she lost consciousness.

WHEN SHE CAME TO she was lying in a field. Tall weeds surrounded her, cutting off the view, and above her the sky was a solid blue. She could feel perspiration on her face and she reached up to brush a damp strand of hair out of her eyes. When she lowered her hand it was dirty, and she stared at it for a moment, somewhat dazed. She felt afraid, but couldn't remember what it was she feared.

Her head was aching and different parts of her body felt sore, bruised. The thought *car accident* was formulating in her mind when the memory of the earthquake jolted her and she suddenly remembered what had happened. Now she knew why she was frightened, and the knowledge made the fear increase.

She got up on her knees in order to see over the weeds. The restaurant was gone, the parking lot was gone, and the landscape, at least what she remembered of it, was considerably changed. Brush-covered hills stretched out as far as she could see, which meant she must have been thrown a second time when she was unconscious, or there had been a field by McDonald's that she had failed to notice.

A few years back there had been a popular song called "A Total Eclipse of the Heart." What occurred to her now was that she had just lived through a total eclipse of the world. There were no signs that there had been an earthquake, but nothing seemed familiar, either. The sirens had stopped and so had the screaming. She seemed to be all alone in an unfamiliar world.

The ache in her head was increasing and she wondered if she had a concussion. A blow to her head might have altered the way she saw things. And yet what she was seeing she was seeing very clearly. She felt thankful to be alive. If the only injury she had sustained was a slight concussion she should consider herself fortunate. She just wished she weren't alone, that help would arrive. Unless they had been swallowed up like the other cars, the highway patrolmen might return. If not them, then at least the local police or the Red Cross—whoever it was that came around after earthquakes and helped those in distress.

She took her Sony Walkman out of her purse and turned the knob to see if she could get any news of the disaster. Nothing came in, not even static, and she finally gave up, leaving it silent, still on her head.

She took out her cigarettes and lit one, and for the first time in her life found herself wishing she had something stronger. With that thought, she suddenly wondered if she was hallucinating. Maybe what she'd thought was health food cereal had been something else, and even now she was only imagining she was sitting in a field, while all the while she was actually still in McDonald's and no doubt acting very strange.

She doubted it, though. She didn't think Mitch would do that to her, not even as a joke—especially when he knew she had to drive. Anyway, she wasn't hearing music, she wasn't seeing colors, she wasn't reacting in slow motion. She closed her eyes for a moment, opened them, pinched herself, and decided she'd go with the earthquake theory.

When it began to appear that no one was going to rescue her, she got to her feet and decided she would have a better chance of being found if she headed for the highway. She had the sick feeling that she was the only one near McDonald's to have survived the quake. The frightening thought that maybe no one else had survived but *her* crossed her mind, but she quickly dismissed it. She had lived through a couple of earthquakes in Southern California when she was growing up and the casualties had never been that bad. Unless, of course, this had been the *major* one, the one the doomsday types were always predicting.

She brushed the dust off her jeans and bent down to retie one of the shoelaces of her Nikes. She was glad her jacket was still intact, but she realized that beneath the jacket she was soaked with sweat, that it was warmer out than it had been before. She didn't know whether earthquakes raised the temperature but thought that must be the case. She took off her jacket and shoved it inside her bag.

Without the McDonald's, without any recognizable landmark, she felt totally disoriented. She couldn't see a highway, she couldn't see any signs of civilization. Only the sun told her which way was west, and she headed in what she believed to be the general direction of San Francisco.

She started off uphill. The terrain was rocky, and she had no idea how far she'd have to go to find a road. When she reached the top of the hill she immediately felt better. The city—or at least its outskirts—appeared in the distance, and she had no doubts that she would be able to make the walk.

She couldn't make out any cars, but then who would be foolish enough to be driving right after an earthquake? She remembered a bad quake that had hit the San Fernando Valley when she was a child. Entire freeways had been shifted and bridges had collapsed. This one couldn't have been too bad, though. At least it didn't appear to have hit the city.

She finally reached a dirt road and headed along it in the lefthand lane. It wasn't much of a road but it was a decided improvement over walking in fields. She kept turning around to see if any cars were coming, hoping to flag one down. Nothing appeared, and after a while she quit looking. It was so quiet she would be able to hear one anyway, and surely after an earthquake the driver would pick up a lone walker, offer some help.

Up ahead on her right she spotted what seemed to be a farm house. She was debating whether or not to throw herself on the owner's mercy or at least ask to use their phone to call a taxi, when coming up behind her she heard the sounds of a car. She crossed to the other side of the road and started to wave her arms as the car came into view.

As it approached her she saw that it was a shiny black convertible with lots of chrome, but she didn't recognize the make. Then, when it stopped a few feet away, she thought it must be one of those antique cars she saw occasionally, the kind people built from kits. Three young men were in it, waving at her.

She walked over to the side of the car to get a better look at them. She wasn't so tired that she was going to go straight from an earthquake into the car of three undesirable characters. They were young, maybe college age, and all dressed up in three-piece suits. Strange-looking suits. They looked as if they were coming from a costume party and had gone as Butch Cassidy and the Sundance Kid. Only there were three of them.

"How bad was it, do you know?" she asked them.

The driver said, "How bad was what?"

"The earthquake. You mean you didn't feel it?"

He shook his head and looked at his friend in the back seat. "I didn't feel an earthquake, did you, Al?"

The young man in the back seat belched. "Not me. But then I guess there could have been one and I would've missed it."

She smelled the liquor on them then and caught sight of the bottle in the front seat. It seemed they were still celebrating New Year's Eve.

The one closer to her in the passenger seat said, "Do you want a ride somewhere?"

Lauren asked, "Are you going into the city?"

There were nods all around.

"I'd appreciate it," she said. "My car got swallowed up in the earthquake you didn't feel."

The man in the passenger seat opened the door, stepped out, then got in the back seat, leaving the front for her.

They started off, and Lauren was about to ask if they would turn on the radio when she saw the car didn't have one. "I was at a McDonald's when it happened," she said, watching uneasily as the three of them passed the bottle back and forth. The driver was obviously in no condition to drive, but since there weren't any other cars on the road she didn't say anything. When they got into the city she'd get out and catch a taxi.

"What's a McDonald's?" asked the driver.

"I don't think you're *that* drunk," remarked Lauren. She reached up to try her own radio again but couldn't get anything in.

"What's that on your head?" asked one of the guys in the back seat.

"It's the new Sony Walkman, haven't you seen it?"

"What does it do?"

She didn't know why they were acting so stupid. "You guys go to college?"

"Berkeley," one of them replied.

"I went to UCLA," she told them.

"Ah, that explains it," said the driver.

"Explains what?"

"Your clothes. They let girls dress like that down there?"

Lauren glanced down at her Mickey Mouse sweatshirt, not answering. Her head was starting to feel a little better but she was in no mood for the silly banter of college boys who had had too much to drink.

"Actually, we thought you were a boy at first."

Lauren, who had never been mistaken for a boy before, let the comment pass. Her chest had been getting enough glances from them and she didn't want to encourage it.

"What does that thing do?" the guy in the back seat was asking again.

"It connects me to people in outer space," Lauren said sarcastically.

"Can I see it?"

She turned around and looked at him and saw that his eyes were riveted to her headphones. She reached into her purse and took out a Bob Seger cassette, inserted it into the Walkman, turned it on and handed the headset to the guy.

He put it on, and as she watched, an expression of horror crossed his face. He ripped off the headset and looked as if he were going to throw it out of the car, but she grabbed it back from him in time.

The three of them were beginning to unnerve her. An earthquake had happened, she was upset enough as it was, and now they wanted to play games with her. She wished some other car had come along first, but theirs was the only one she had even seen so far. They must really be driving the back roads.

"There was music coming out of that thing," the guy was saying, awe in his voice.

The driver's glance moved back and forth between Lauren and his friend, then he pulled the car over to the side of the road and stopped. "Let me see that," he said to her, holding out his hand.

Afraid to do otherwise, Lauren handed the set to him and watched as he put it on his head. He listened for a few seconds, then took it off. "What in hell *is* this?"

"Look, you guys are drunk, maybe I better walk," suggested Lauren, reaching for the door handle.

"I might be drunk, but I still want to know what this is."

"Give me a break, will you?" she said. There had been an earthquake, people had been killed, and all they could do was joke around. Still, she needed the ride. In an effort to pacify them, she went on, "All right, so you guys are probably into hard rock. I apologize. I happen to like Seger."

He handed the headset to her. "We said we'd give you a ride and we will. You're pretty strange, though, you know it? I was in Los Angeles once and I don't remember the people being that odd."

Lauren decided that not only were they drunk, they must be *on* something. She put the headset back in her purse so it wouldn't aggravate them any further, then took out her cigarettes. Trying to make it up with them, she passed the pack around.

"What're these things on the end of the cigarettes?" asked one of the guys in the back.

"It's called a filter," said Lauren. "Something missing from the kind of cigarettes *you* smoke, I imagine."

"What's it for?"

"Will you get serious?" she retorted. "If you don't want one, pass 'em back."

She leaned over to shield herself from the wind as she lit her cigarette. She was beginning to think this must be some kind of fraternity stunt. They had probably been forced to dress up in those out-of-date clothes, given the old car to drive, and told to go out and pick up hitchhikers and drive them crazy. If so, they were succeeding.

"Won't this thing go any faster?" Lauren asked after a while. At the rate they were going they wouldn't hit the city before nightfall.

"I'm going twenty," said the driver.

"I know you're going twenty. How about going forty? I realize this isn't a freeway, but still..."

He laughed and turned around to repeat what she'd said to the guys in the back seat, as if doing forty were some kind of joke. It was then that she saw the horse and wagon pull out onto the road. She was about to yell "Watch out!" when the car hit the horse and she let out a scream.

"Oh, God," groaned the driver, righting the car and continuing down the road, his face white. "*Now* we're in for it."

"Aren't you even going to stop?" demanded Lauren, horrified at what had happened. She turned around to see the driver climbing out of the ditch, waving his fists at them.

"My father will *kill* me when he hears about this," said the driver.

"We'll make sure he *doesn't* hear about it," one of his friends reassured him.

Lauren noticed that her hand was shaking. This all felt like some kind of nightmare she couldn't wake up from. First the earthquake, then these strange guys. She closed her eyes and rested her head on the car door, wishing she could just get home and give her parents a call to tell them she was all right. She didn't think she could take much more of these spoiled boys.

A little while later the driver said, "Where do you want us to take you?"

She opened her eyes and gazed around. They appeared to be in the city, except everything looked so different she had trouble recognizing it. Some of the buildings were the same, some had changed, and the streets were all dirt. What's more, the people she saw were dressed like the young men in the car. All the men were wearing three-piece suits with hats, and all the women were wearing long dresses. And the craziest thing of all, the streets were filled with horses and buggies. The only normal thing she saw was a streetcar, and even that didn't seem quite the same.

"What is this? Are they filming a movie in San Francisco?"

"A what?" asked the driver.

"Look, what's going on?" said Lauren.

"All I asked is where you want me to take you. Where do you live?"

"Near Union Street," she told him.

"Where near Union Street?"

She gave him the address, then asked, "Why's everyone dressed like that?"

"Like what?"

"Like it's a hundred years ago!" She was losing patience with their weird sense of humor.

"Lady, just because *you* dress strange, don't expect everyone else to."

And that's what was so peculiar. She was the only one dressed in jeans and a sweatshirt.

"What is this, the city celebrating Old San Francisco Days or something?"

She overheard a comment in the back seat about her being a foreigner, and she turned around. "No, I'm no foreigner, I just want to know what's going on. First the earthquake, now this—I'm beginning to feel like I'm going crazy."

She could swear the driver edged away from her. Maybe they were right, maybe she was crazy. Or maybe the entire thing was a hallucination. The only way she could credit that was if Mitch had doctored her cereal with something pretty strong. And if this was what happened on recreational pharmaceuticals, she was very glad she'd thus far avoided them.

She started paying more attention to the area they were driving through and realized that something was very, very wrong. According to the street signs they had just passed Union Square, and the only thing familiar about it was the square itself. Macy's wasn't there, nor was Saks or Neiman-Marcus or any of the other stores she shopped in. There were buildings all right, but none she'd ever seen before.

There wasn't one movie theater, one boutique, one book store, one fast food place. And everywhere she looked people were dressed in funny clothes and riding in horse-drawn buggies. When occasionally she did spot a car, it was always an old one, like the one she was riding in.

Something bizarre had to be going on—like a movie company taking over the entire city to make a period film. But surely the cost would be prohibitive to hire this many extras. Maybe it was Woody Allen having his ultimate revenge on California.

The guys were being awfully quiet. She had a feeling she frightened them in some way, but she couldn't figure out why. There were three of them and only one of her.

Trying to lighten things up, she said, "This *is* the twentieth century, isn't it?"

"I'll drink to that," said the driver, taking a long pull from the bottle before handing it back to the others. "Happy 1906, everyone."

Lauren did a double take. "Happy *what*?"

The driver looked over at her. "1906. Where have you been, anyway? You sleep through New Year's or something?"

"Very funny," she said.

When he pulled up in front of the building and parked, Lauren got out. It wasn't her building, but she'd just as soon walk as stay any longer with those nuts. "Thanks for the ride," she told them, then watched them drive off, relieved to be rid of them.

She tried to get her bearings, then noticed that the number on the door of the house was the same as the number where she lived. They must've let her off at the wrong street.

She slipped her bag over her shoulder and walked to the corner to take a look at the street signs. When they matched up, she was at a loss. She walked around the neighborhood, examining each building carefully. Some she recognized, some she didn't. She'd only been gone two weeks. It wasn't conceivable that so many people could have renovated their buildings in that time—and renovated them to look *old*.

She decided to head down to Union Street and check out some of the places where her friends hung out. One of them would be able to tell her what was happening. And if the earthquake hadn't hit the city, maybe she'd better report it to the police. It might have struck only the area she'd been in, and maybe they weren't even aware of it yet.

Union Street was the weirdest of all. Gone were the trendy shops and galleries; gone was Doidge's, where she often had Sunday brunch; gone was Crane & Kelley, where she frequently went for take-out; gone was Perry's, where she usually did her drinking. Instead, and this was the hardest to figure of all, she could swear that what she was seeing were dairies. Not that she had ever seen a real dairy, but she was seeing cows. Real live *cows*. On *Union Street*!

She got out of there fast, walking back toward Union Square as quickly as she could. She ignored the stares of passersby and was almost running by the time she reached downtown. Only when she saw a boy selling newspapers did she come to a halt.

She stopped and stared at the headlines. They were strange, unfamiliar: Striving for downfall of Count Witte . . . Game rooster attacks girl . . . Wed me or I will shoot myself.

It was the *San Francisco Chronicle*, all right, but she'd never seen it like this before.

Then she noticed the date on the paper and felt her stomach turn over. It said: Monday, January 1, 1906.

Chapter One

Mayor Eugene Schmitz was quoted today as saying that all indications are that 1906 will turn into an ever-increasingly prosperous year for the citizenry of our fair city.

—*San Francisco Chronicle*, Monday, Jan. 1, 1906

LAUREN STOOD on the street corner, trembling, until the newsboy asked her if anything was wrong.

She looked at him and just shook her head. It wasn't one thing that was wrong, it was everything.

"That's a funny shirt you're wearing," he said, his eyes on Mickey Mouse.

She realized it *was* a funny shirt—peculiar funny. Putting down her duffel bag, she unzipped it, took out her leather jacket and slipped it on. "How much is a paper?" she asked the kid.

"Five cents, same as always."

She pulled her wallet out and searched inside for a nickel. It was kind of dark out. Maybe he wouldn't notice that the coin didn't have a buffalo on it or whatever it should have had on it in 1906. She gave it to him and he put it in his pocket without so much as a glance, handing her one of the papers.

She shoved it into her duffel bag. She didn't want to read it. Mostly she wanted it as a souvenir in case the world suddenly righted itself and everything went back to normal again.

She kept thinking this all had to be a dream and any minute she'd wake up. Time travel? Hell, she didn't even believe in astrology!

Time travel wasn't something she could come to terms with. She never read science fiction and the only thing she knew about time travel was a movie she'd seen years ago, but that had been about scientists and a time machine, and they'd gone forward in time, not back.

All she could deduce was that the earthquake must have been such a strong one that even time had been thrown out of kilter. She wouldn't have believed something like that was possible, except the evidence was right before her eyes. If she hadn't stopped at McDonald's, if she'd just driven straight home, none of this would've happened. She'd been in the wrong place at the wrong time, and now she was stuck.

Suddenly it dawned on her that no one would believe her. Why should they? She wouldn't believe such a crazy story herself. What it amounted to was that she was in a strange place where she knew no one, where her money and credit cards were of no value, and where she didn't even have a place to sleep that night. If she tried to explain her predicament to anyone, she'd no doubt be locked up in a mental institution. And she had the feeling that mental institutions in 1906 were not the kind of places she'd want to be.

She had to do something. She didn't fancy sleeping in the street, and maybe it was illegal in 1906. She couldn't even sleep in the BART station because there was no longer a BART. What she needed was an ally, someone who would believe in her. But she knew such a person wouldn't be easy to find. Maybe not even possible to find.

She thought of the police, of newspapers, even scientists. Her normal instinct would be to go to the police and try to explain the situation to them, but she was afraid they'd be the first to think her out of her mind and lock her up. The newspapers were a possibility. But even if she convinced some reporter that she was who she said she was, he'd probably write her up as some kind of freak.

Maybe a church. Weren't churches supposed to take in people who had nowhere else to go? Surely the times were modern enough that she wouldn't be considered a witch or some other kind of undesirable. Somehow, though, she thought she trusted the churches even less than the police. They would probably think the way she was *dressed* was sacrilegious.

She noticed it was getting darker and she put her sunglasses away in her purse. Shifting the bag to her other shoulder, she cursed the fact that the city was built on hills. It was hard enough driving around; walking was murder.

She needed a drink. What she really, desperately needed was a drink. Were there bars in 1906? Was prohibition in effect then? She didn't think so; it came later, maybe in the twenties. But history had never been her strong suit. If there were bars, she was pretty sure they wouldn't allow women in them. Then again, if the bar was dark enough, she might pass for a man. She hadn't seen any women in pants while she'd been walking. And any makeup she might have put on that morning was long gone. Her hair was short enough that she could pass for a young man in need of a haircut. Yes, what she needed was a bar. A place to sit down. A drink to calm her nerves. Maybe some information on where she could get a room for the night. A cheap room. A place where they might not look too carefully at her money.

Oh, *God*—if she wasn't careful all of this was going to seem like a game. The thing was, nothing felt real, and it was becoming hard to take her predicament seriously. She had the strange feeling that just like in a dream, she could do anything she wanted and it wouldn't matter. She could say or do the most outrageous things, and somehow she wouldn't be accountable. Because this wasn't *her* world, was it? Her world had disappeared.

One thing she was thankful for: if she had to leave her own time, she was glad she'd been thrown back and not forward. She didn't think she'd be able to cope with a more modern age, but the only good thing about going back in time was that she would know more than anyone else. In fact she knew more about the future than anyone else alive in the world today. If she'd paid more attention in history class when she was in school, was more conversant with the period, she'd be able to set herself up as a fortune teller. Or a prophet. As it was, she didn't even know who the president was in 1906.

She noticed a bar up ahead and quickened her pace. When she got to the window she peered inside and saw that the bar itself was lined with men. The place looked suitably dark, though, and it also appeared warm and inviting. She scanned the room carefully but didn't see a woman anywhere. Which might be just as well. She had a feeling that women were going to be more outraged at the way she dressed than men.

Ordinarily she wouldn't have walked into such a bar alone. But then, these weren't ordinary times to her. She opened the door and stepped inside. Most of the light was over the door, so she walked a few feet forward until she blended into the shadows. There was no music, but the place was noisy with talk. She saw right away it didn't attract a young crowd—hardly the kind of singles bar she was used to. But then it wasn't a gay bar, either. And that was a novelty in San Francisco, or at least it was in her day.

There were a couple of empty spots at the bar and she picked the one where the occupants on either side seemed to be minding their own business. Setting the duffel bag down, she took a seat. The bartender was at the far end of the counter engrossed in conversation. If she wanted a drink she'd have to shout at him, and that didn't seem like a good idea.

The men on either side of her ignored her. On her right sat a white-haired man who looked quite drunk. He was muttering to himself, then pausing as if he heard someone else reply. Only no one was talking to him. On her left was a man of about forty, lean and dark, hunched over his drink as though it were serious business.

What suddenly struck her was that the people here smelled. She'd been vaguely aware of it before but hadn't put words to the impression. The boys in the car had smelled, but at the time she'd put it down to a weekend of partying. In the close confines of the bar, however, besides the smoke and the liquor, she could smell the men. Didn't people bathe in 1906? Was deodorant a later invention?

She knew the bartender would notice her presence soon and come down the bar to take her order. She was hesitant to spend the little money she had and doubtful whether it would pass inspection anyway. Without even thinking about what she was going to say first, she leaned toward the dark man and said in a low voice near his ear, "If you'll buy me a drink, I'll give you the opportunity of experiencing something you've never experienced before." She instantly regretted her action as the ambiguity of the words hit home.

The man lurched forward a little on his bar stool, then, without even looking at her, replied, "There's nothing I haven't experienced." He added, more to himself than to her, "However, I admire your style."

Lauren began to smile. "I'll tell you what. If you find it isn't a new experience, I'll buy *you* a drink."

He still didn't look at her. "Is it a wager, then?"

She nodded, then realized he couldn't see the nod. "Yes, a wager. You on?"

He tilted his head in her direction, turning it slightly so that she could see one dark, bloodshot eye. "Is this something that can be experienced right here? Because I have to be honest, I don't think I'd get too far walking."

"Right here," Lauren told him, reaching into her bag for the Sony Walkman. She decided Bob Seger might be too much of a new experience and instead took out a Willie Nelson cassette. She set it on his head and he winced a little. "Now don't worry—this isn't going to hurt," she assured him. Then she turned it on.

He sat upright on the bar stool, his eyes fixed on hers. But he didn't freak out the way the guys in the car had. He just sat there, looking as though he didn't believe what he was hearing.

She figured he'd heard enough for her to win the wager, and anyway, she didn't want the batteries to wear out too fast. Because once they wore out, that was the end of her music. Forever.

She took the set off his head and put it out of sight again in her purse. "Well, do I get a drink?"

He was studying her closely now, his eyes sweeping her face. "You're a female, aren't you?"

"Does it matter?"

He managed a lopsided smile. "Not to me. But don't let Charlie get too close a look at you. Women aren't allowed in here. What're you having?"

"A beer would be fine."

"Hey, Charlie," he yelled down the bar, "another whiskey for me and a beer for my friend."

Lauren kept her head down while the drinks were brought to them, then relaxed when the bartender returned to the end of the counter, where he appeared to be in deep discussion with a group of men. The label on the bottle said Cascade. She drank down half of the beer, then took out her cigarettes and lighter. She offered one to her new friend, who was eyeing the disposable lighter with curiosity.

"Another trick?" he asked.

Which gave her the idea for a second career opportunity. She could pose as a magician as well as a fortune teller. It was for damn sure she wasn't going to find a job as a computer systems analyst in 1906.

She shook her head. "No trick."

He ignored her pack and reached for his own. They were called Turkish Trophies and were unfiltered. He put one in his mouth and she held out the lighter, but he raised his hand to block her.

"Hold on a minute," he said. "What does it do? More music?"

Lauren lit her own cigarette with her Bic and watched his astonished expression. She was beginning to enjoy this new power to surprise.

"Want me to light yours?" she asked.

"Let me see you do that again."

She clicked the lighter on and off a couple of times, then put it in his outstretched hand.

"What do you call this?"

"I call it a lighter."

"You're full of surprises, and here I thought it was going to be a dull evening." He got the hang of the lighter on the first try, then flicked it on and off a few times before passing it back to her. "Got a name?"

"Lauren."

He was smiling now, his eyes almost shut. "Even your name's different. Are you real or am I so drunk I'm imagining all this?"

"I don't know," said Lauren. "Maybe I'm not real. Maybe none of this is real."

"That's what I figured," he said, leaning back over his drink.

She finished her beer and wished she had another. "What's your name?" she asked him, suddenly eager to hear his voice again.

"Early Cruz."

And he thought *her* name was different? "Listen, Mr. Cruz, could I ask your advice on something?"

"You can try."

"I need a place to stay."

"Plenty of hotels around. And rooming houses. Take your pick."

"Do you know of anyplace around here?"

He turned back to her. "Lots of places around here. How particular are you? You need electricity? Running water?"

She hadn't even thought about those things not being included. "How much would a place like that cost?"

He shrugged. "Anywhere from a dollar and a quarter a week to about three dollars."

"That cheap."

"Well, we're not talking about the St. Francis..."

Lauren avoided his eyes. "The thing is . . . I don't have any money. At least not any money they'd take at a hotel."

"Foreign currency?"

"I guess you could say that."

"I tell you what, Lauren. I know the night clerk over at the Belmont House, corner of Sutter and Jones. Tell Jimmy I sent you and that you'll pay as soon as you can get your currency changed at a bank."

"You've been very kind and I thank you. I wonder . . . would you buy me another beer if I showed you something else?"

His eyes narrowed. "What've you got up your sleeve now?"

"If I show you something you've never seen before, will you buy me another?"

He gave a bark of laughter. "I'll buy you one anyway."

But when the beer came, he said, "Truth to tell, I wouldn't mind seeing another of your tricks."

Lauren took her pocket calculator out of her purse and set it on the bar in front of him. "See this?"

"Yeah, I'm watching."

She pressed some numbers then looked over at him.

"I'm still watching," he said.

She totalled them. "Did you see that?"

"Yeah, I saw it, but I don't believe it."

"Try it yourself," she said.

He imitated what she'd done, then swore out loud when the total appeared on the tiny screen. "I don't know what that is or how it works," he told her, "but I bet you could exchange it for any room in town." He leaned closer to her and squinted, as though trying to size her up. "I also don't know where you come from or what you are, but if you're not a figment of my drunken state, then you truly are amazing."

Lauren laughed out loud, noticing too late that her laughter had attracted Charlie. He came down the length of the bar and took a good look at her, leaning over the counter so far she could smell the whiskey on his breath. She could see that other men in the place were aware of her now, also.

He said to Early Cruz, "I'm going to have to ask your friend to leave, Early. You know we don't allow women in here."

"Now, Charlie—"

"Rules is rules, Early. Sorry, miss, but you're going to have to go."

"I was just leaving," said Lauren, finishing off the beer and climbing down from the stool. She picked up her duffel bag, then turned to Early Cruz.

"Thanks for the beers," she told him.

He gave a nod. "Thanks for the interesting dream."

She found the Belmont House not far from Union Square. It looked fine from the outside—small, but not so small she'd stand out. She walked through the front door and into a small lobby with stuffed velvet chairs and an overhead electrical fixture. The only person around was the young man at the registration desk.

She went over to the counter. "Are you Jimmy?"

"That's my name," he replied, making an obvious effort not to stare at her clothes.

She tried to sound self-confident. "Early Cruz recommended that I stay here. Do you have any rooms available?"

"We have several available," he told her.

She crossed her fingers. "I have a problem. My money is all in French francs and I couldn't get it changed at the bank today because of the holiday.

He looked genuinely sorry. "I'm afraid the hotel has a pay-in-advance policy."

"What I was thinking," Lauren began, trying to act very casual, "is that maybe you'd take something of mine in lieu of money. Or just as a deposit until I get some."

"What did you have in mind?"

Well, at least he hadn't given her an outright no. She pushed up the sleeve of her leather jacket and showed him her digital watch. It was a cheap Japanese model; her grandmother had given her a new watch for Christmas that she much preferred.

"I don't believe I've ever seen anything like that," he said, his eyes riveted to her watch.

"They're new," she told him, "the latest thing from Switzerland. You never have to wind them."

He was clearly fascinated by the watch, and she moved her arm closer to him so he could get a better look.

"What's something like that worth?" he asked her.

"About fifty dollars, but I'd be willing to trade it for...two weeks' stay in the hotel," she said, hoping to strike a quick bargain.

The young man seemed torn between his duty and the watch. "Do you think we could make a private deal here?"

"What did you have in mind?" asked Lauren, knowing she had him hooked.

"I have some money I could spare. I'd be quite willing to pay for you to have two weeks here in return for the watch."

Lauren, who knew he was getting the best of the bargain, agreed. "Thank you, and I truly appreciate it."

He pushed the register across to her and she signed Lauren Hall, giving her parents' address in Los Angeles. When he saw what she'd written, he commented, "Oh, you're from Los Angeles," as though that explained why she looked so different.

Not wanting to be drawn into a conversation, Lauren thanked him again, then took the proffered key and climbed the stairs to her third-floor room.

The room turned out to have electricity, but the bulb hanging from the ceiling must have been two watts at most. There was a small sink with running water but no toilet or tub, and she assumed those would be found down the hall. At least she hoped they'd be there. There was a large, soft-looking bed, a dresser, an upholstered chair and a wardrobe. The walls were papered in a dark floral pattern, giving the room a gloomy air.

In an effort to assess her situation, she put her bag on the bed and unzipped it, then removed one item at a time. She hadn't taken many clothes with her to Los Angeles, and what she had didn't look at all suitable for San

Francisco in 1906. Not that she was about to wear dresses that went down to the ground, but she didn't want to attract too much attention to herself, either.

She had a Naf Naf jumpsuit in olive drab and the belt that went with it, which was made to look like a gun belt. There was a second jumpsuit in red silk that she'd worn on Christmas, an extra pair of Levi's, some gray Guess pants with lots of pockets and a matching vest, and assorted T-shirts and sweatshirts. She had also packed her bikini, which probably would be useless except perhaps as underwear, a white nylon parka with a hood, some bras and pants and a couple of nightgowns. In a plastic bag she found her black leather boots and a pair of red sandals.

She put the clothes away in the wardrobe. Every item she'd packed would only make her stand out in a crowd. She thought of cutting her hair and posing as a boy, but wearing a 34B bra wouldn't help that charade. And anyway, she didn't want to be a boy. In fact she didn't want to be in 1906 at all.

She opened her cosmetic case and took out her travel hair dryer, then searched the room for electrical outlets. Finding none, she shoved the dryer back in her duffle bag. She had shampoo, vitamins, a toothbrush, a half-filled tube of Aim, a deodorant stick and a brush and comb. She arranged these items on the shelf above the sink, then dumped the contents of her purse onto the bed.

Each item seemed to offer possibilities for trade. There was the pocket calculator that Early had found so interesting, an address book and two ballpoint pens, her car

and apartment keys on a plastic key holder that adver-
tised the 1984 Summer Games in Los Angeles, four cassettes, a packet of Kleenex, a paperback mystery, the
latest *People* magazine, her cigarettes, her Bic, a book of
matches from a restaurant in L.A. and her birth control
pills.

If only she were a chemist, she thought wryly, she
could make a fortune producing birth control pills. She'd
probably even become famous. Opening the plastic container, she saw that she had eighteen more days in her life
when she could safely have sex. If she'd known at the
time what was in store for her, she might not have insisted on sleeping on Mitch's couch.

A velvet pouch contained her new watch, two pairs of
gold earrings, a gold chain and a ring with a gold Mexican peso. If she had to, she could probably sell the gold
jewelry.

Her cosmetic case held what was probably the only
blush, lipstick, eye liner and eye shadow in existence.
And none of them were going to last her beyond another
month. She was doomed to become the natural type
whether she liked it or not.

The last items in her purse were her sunglasses, which
she set on the dresser, her checkbook and her wallet. She
opened the wallet and saw her driver's license, a couple
of credit cards, her Macy's charge card, some of her
business cards, a health insurance card, a snapshot of her
parents and exactly $63.87.

She knew she had a lot of thinking to do, a lot of
planning, but the beer and all the walking she'd done, to

say nothing of the events of the day, had made her both physically and mentally exhausted.

Spotting towels on the shelf of the wardrobe, she decided to check out the bathroom and then go to bed. It was down the hall from her room, where she'd guessed it would be. Thankfully it contained both a flush toilet and a tub. She'd been hoping there were such things as flush toilets.

Unfortunately, she found that running water meant cold water, and she didn't stay in the bathroom long. Back in her room, she put on one of her nightgowns and got into bed, leaving the overhead light on.

Used to reading a little before she went to sleep, she opened the paper and glanced through it. On page two she read that the Roosevelt family had returned to the capital, then continued reading and learned that Theodore Roosevelt was president. She couldn't remember one single thing about him.

The advertisements were amusing. There were "Up-to-Date Walking Shoes" for $1.85, suits for men on sale for $35 and corset covers for only fifty cents. On the sports page she saw a picture of the Olympic Club athletes taking their year-end swim in the most ridiculous looking bathing suits she'd ever seen.

There was a large classified section and she was heartened to see a Female Help Wanted column. She'd been afraid that women didn't work. None of the jobs looked suitable for her, though. Some of them involved work on sewing machines, there were a couple for stenographers, one for a hairdresser and the majority for maids and housework. The salaries ranged from $10 to $25, and she assumed that meant per week. Well, if she had to, she supposed she could do housework. The only problem would be in getting a woman to hire her, looking the way she did.

What surprised her most was that there were personal ads, and the majority of them sounded like people conducting illicit affairs. A Karl Etier was advertising that he paid cash for diamonds, and she decided to keep him in mind for her gold.

The light was weak and her eyes grew tired, so she put the paper on the floor, pulled the covers up to her chin, and tried to relax so that sleep would come. Then, just when she was sure it might, the thought that had lain unbidden in her mind for the last few hours surfaced, and she felt tears forming in her eyes. It was the thought that she would never know what had happened to her parents. She would never know how bad the earthquake had been or whether they had survived. And if they had, they would know by now that she hadn't, since she'd promised to call them as soon as she arrived home.

She wasn't a kid, by any means. She was an adult of 31 and used to taking care of herself. But she'd always counted on her family being around for a long time, and the thought that she might be causing them untold anguish made the tears begin to flow. So okay, she was being a crybaby, and she detested crybabies. She couldn't help it. She'd loved her job, and that was gone. She had good friends she'd never see again. She'd never see another Clint Eastwood picture, or read another book by

Warren Murphy, or see the Forty-Niners play, or watch *Saturday Night Live* on television. Nothing was ever going to be the same again, and right now, at this very moment in time—1906 time, to be exact—she felt she was entitled to a good cry.

Tomorrow she'd be brave.

Chapter Two

WEARING JEANS, her black leather jacket and boots, her curly hair slicked back with water, Lauren sat on a bench in Union Square, looking at the morning edition of the *Chronicle* she'd found in the lobby.

It was the first paper of the new year and one of the headlines immediately caught her eye: Says Scorchers Wrecked Buggy. She didn't know what a scorcher was, but the wrecked buggy sounded all too familiar. With a sense of foreboding she read on.

An immense "black devil" automobile containing a party of four men and running at a fast clip crashed into a horse and wagon yesterday afternoon. The horse was killed and the rig sustained injuries. John Walsh, a farmer, was thrown into a ditch by the roadside but escaped serious injury. The automobilists put on full steam and proceeded on their journey, apparently heading for the city. Walsh swore to a complaint against them and a description of the machine and party was telegraphed to the chief of police here. Three hours later a car answering the description of that wanted, and driven by Walter Scott Martin, a student at Berkeley College, who was accompanied by two other students, was stopped by the police and the whole party taken into custody. A description of the fourth party was given the police by Martin, but the officer who talked to this reporter said that the description was bizarre and that it wasn't given credence by the police. Anyone knowing the name or the whereabouts of

the suspected fourth party is asked to notify the authorities.

Through no fault of her own, the police were now
looking for her. She could just imagine the bizarre description. The boys probably had told the police about
her strange clothes and the funny thing she wore over her
ears. And if the description got out, there would be other
people who had seen her and would be able to describe
her to the police. She feared she would be found quickly
in a city where she was the only female in pants.

She considered going to the police, then thought better of it. It would do her little good to be locked up when
she didn't even have the means to hire a lawyer. Were
there paupers' prisons in 1906? If there were, she had no
desire to reside in one. And she didn't think the police
would believe she just happened to be from another time,
thrown back into theirs quite by accident.

The newspaper might be a better bet. She had a much
greater regard for the intelligence of newspaper people.
She had proof they might pay attention to, and if they
had her story and the police did manage to pick her up,
at least she might get a fair hearing in the press.

Anyway, she couldn't think of anything better to do,
and a walk over to the *Chronicle* offices might take her
mind off her hunger. She had approached a couple of
restaurants in order to get some breakfast but had chick-
ened out at the last moment. She was afraid that trying
to spend the kind of money she had might be against the
law, and she didn't want to encounter any trouble before
she had a game plan in mind. It occurred to her that from

now on her life might have to be run on a series of game plans.

She found the address in the newspaper, then walked over to the Chronicle Building on the corner of Market and Kearny streets. The building not only looked new, it appeared to be the largest one around. Pretending more self-confidence than she felt, she entered the lobby and went to the information desk. She showed the article to the man in charge and told him it was urgent that she speak to the reporter who wrote the story.

"That'd be Maddox," said the man, hardly bothering to look at her. "He'd be in the newsroom."

"Where would—"

He pointed her in the direction, and she took off down the hall. The newsroom looked just the way she'd always pictured a newsroom to look. It was filled with men, their jackets off and shirt sleeves rolled up, but what was missing was the sound of typewriters. Those men who appeared to be working at all were seated at wooden desks writing in longhand. Obviously the typewriter hadn't gained much popularity, at least not with newsmen.

She asked the man nearest her where she could find Maddox, and he shouted out, "Maddox." But at that moment she spotted Early Cruz. He was one of a group of men standing around talking. A cigarette stuck out the side of his mouth, and as he spoke, he gestured with his hands.

Not even bothering to look for Maddox any longer, Lauren walked over to where Cruz was standing and waited for a moment while he finished what he was saying. Off the bar stool he was taller than she had imagined, but then he had been slouched on the stool. He was very tall and very lean and still as dark as he had appeared in the dim bar. The "Cruz" would probably account for that, although she didn't think he looked Mexican.

Then, warned by the stares she was getting from his companions, he turned around and saw her. His mouth started to drop open, but he clamped it shut just in time to prevent the cigarette from dropping out.

"Do you remember me, Mr. Cruz?" she asked.

Without a word of greeting, he grabbed her arm and hustled her over to a desk in front of one of the windows. He practically shoved her into a chair, then took a seat behind the desk. "You" was all he could say.

"You remember me then?"

"I swear to God, I thought I imagined you. How'd you find me? I don't remember telling you where I worked."

"I had no idea you'd be here, but since you are . . . I could really use your help again."

He was staring at her and shaking his head. "More tricks?"

She took a deep breath, wishing he looked happier to see her. Still, he was a familiar face. "I'm in really bad trouble, so bad I don't know what to do," she told him.

"Didn't the hotel work out?"

"The hotel was fine, Mr. Cruz."

"So what's the problem?"

"It's a long story, and I don't know whether you'll believe me. I guess if I were you, I wouldn't believe me." She was beginning to think that approaching him had been a bad idea. In the clear light of day he didn't look kind or benign or even particularly friendly. In fact, there was a dangerous air about him. She had been foolish to think he would help her. No one was going to help her. No one was even going to believe her.

He was consulting a gold pocket watch. "You had lunch?"

She shook her head. "I haven't even had breakfast."

"Didn't get that foreign currency of yours changed yet?"

"That's part of the problem."

He didn't appear to be taking her seriously, because he grinned then and said, "Show me another trick and I'll buy you lunch." But the grin was mocking and held no mirth.

"Please..."

"Come on—I want to prove to myself that what I remember happening last night did happen."

Feeling as though she were in the sideshow of a circus, Lauren opened her purse and debated what she should pull out next. She finally handed him one of her ballpoint pens.

"What's this?" he asked.

"It's a pen. Go on, try it."

"Doesn't look like any pen I've ever seen."

"I know. But it works."

He tried to write with it but nothing happened.

"You have to press down on the end first," she instructed.

Then he was writing with it, amazement and skepticism blending on his face. "Where'd you get this?"

"That's what I want to talk to you about, Mr. Cruz."

"You might as well call me Early, seeing as I don't even know your last name."

"It's Hall."

"Okay, Lauren Hall, let's go to lunch."

He took her down the street to a restaurant crowded with mostly men, though she did see a couple of tables of women. He ordered for them both, and when the lunches came—roast chicken and vegetables—they were hearty and flavorful. It was more than Lauren usually ate for lunch, but she was starving and had no trouble finishing the meal off. They didn't talk while they ate, and Early drank steadily the whole time. He still appeared sober, though, when they had finished and she was drinking coffee: very good coffee, albeit strong.

"You ready to tell me that story now?" he asked her, leaning back in his chair, a gold toothpick residing in the space between his front teeth.

Lauren had run out of cigarettes and asked him for one. It was strong, but it tasted good. She put the morning's newspaper in front of him and pointed to the article in question. "I'm the fourth party, the one the police are looking for."

His eyes scanned the piece. "That's Maddox's story."

"I know it is. I went there to see him, but then I recognized you. Anyway, I have a lot more problems than just that story."

He wrapped his foot around the chair leg and tilted himself back, looking at her with narrowed eyes. "Want to tell me about it?"

"They picked me up and gave me a ride into the city. I was with them when they hit the horse, but I couldn't do anything about it. They were just kids and were afraid to stop."

"I guess you are in a little trouble."

"That's not the half of it, Mr. Cruz."

"If you want my help, I'm going to have to insist you call me Early."

"I don't think you're going to believe this, Early, but I don't belong here. Look, I really don't know how to explain this." She reached into her purse and pulled out her wallet. She removed her driver's license and handed it to him.

"That picture's in color" was the first thing he said.

"Yes. And please note the dates on the license."

He seemed to read it for a long time. Then he started to smile. "It says you were born in 1955."

"I was."

He sat there as though waiting for the punch line.

"Early, I don't know how or why, except there was an earthquake that I think was probably pretty strong . . . yesterday at this time I was living in 1987. And I swear to you, I'm not crazy."

"I need another drink. You want a drink?"

She started to shake her head, then changed her mind. "Yeah, I'll have a beer."

He called over a waiter, gave the order, then sat there and stared at her until the drinks came. He raised his glass to her, and something about his attitude made her think he had to be drunk to listen to her.

"What you're telling me is that you're from another time, correct?"

She nodded.

"Don't you think I'd have to be a little crazy to believe you?"

"But look at me. Do I look like any of the women you know? Have you ever seen a pen like that before, or a cigarette lighter, or the calculator I showed you last night? Have you ever seen a color picture before? Have you ever heard music like the music I played for you?"

"I don't believe in stuff like that. Traveling back in time."

Lauren sighed. "I don't, either. At least I didn't before."

"You got any other proof?"

"Quite a bit. But it could all be tricks, I guess."

"Pretty good tricks, I'd say."

She took out all the money from her wallet and spread it on the table in front of him. "Look at the dates on it," she said.

He spent a long time examining the money while she reached over and took another of his cigarettes. If only he'd believe; if only he would help her.

He finally looked up from the money. "Why'd you have to pick on me? Of all the thousands of men in San Francisco, why me?"

"I'm sorry. There wasn't anyone else."

"I don't have time to get mixed up with some crazy lady who says—"

"I'm sorry, I made a mistake..."

He finished off his drink in one gulp then bent over, his elbows on the table, his face hidden from her. "Get away from me, Lauren Hall—I don't need this kind of trouble. Go back to wherever you came from."

Close to tears of frustration, Lauren gathered up her money and shoved everything back in her purse. She stood and said, "Thank you for the lunch, Mr. Cruz," then waited for a minute to see if he would change his mind. When he continued to ignore her, she turned and made her way through the crowded restaurant and out the door.

Once on the street she hesitated, wondering what to do next. She had to get organized. She had to do something to help herself and not try to rely on strangers. People in 1906 appeared to be as unwilling to get involved as people in the eighties. She had always felt she was self-sufficient, independent, liberated. It had been against her nature to ask Early Cruz for help. But for the life of her, she couldn't think what to do next.

She began to walk. The business area was crowded so she headed in the opposite direction, crossing dirt streets, avoiding the numerous horses and buggies. There didn't appear to be any order to the traffic movement: no stop signs, no lights, no policemen directing people. Because she was wearing pants she was able to make her way successfully, but she didn't know how women in skirts managed.

And because of the horses the streets were filthy, making it necessary to look down with every step. The smell was horrendous. People in her time might complain about cars and trucks polluting the air, but she would gladly take automobile exhaust over these smells any day. And there was air pollution around, anyway, judging by the black smoke she saw billowing out of the chimneys of buildings.

She passed by a small park and entered. Women were pushing babies in elaborate carriages, and a few small children were running around. Lauren found an empty bench and sat down, ignoring the curious stares of the other women. She opened the newspaper she was carrying and turned to the classified section. Her first priority was to find work. Without money, there was no way she was going to be able to survive.

She knew nothing about sewing or sewing machines, so quickly skipped over those ads. She could type well enough, at least on computers, but every office job required stenography, and she didn't know the first thing about that. She was also sure that office jobs would require recommendations, if not experience. It was going to have to be housework, much as she hated the idea.

There were a few jobs for "second maids," but they sounded as though they were in large establishments, so she ignored them. Several families wanted women to do housework or care for children, but when she looked over at the other side of the page to Situations Wanted Women, she saw there were ten times as many experienced women seeking jobs as there were jobs being offered. And most of these jobs required letters of reference.

What woman in her right mind would hire her, looking the way she did? She wouldn't. She wouldn't want some nut in her house who said she was from 1987.

WALDENBOOKS

```
SALE        1270   11  1502   01/05/88
                      60      17:32

0373970420                      3.95
               SUBTOTAL         3.95
GEORGIA  3.0% TAX                .12
               TOTAL            4.07
               CHECK            4.07
           PV#0015680
    AMERICA FINDS IT AT WALDENBOOKS
```

She got up off the bench and decided to go back to the hotel. At least she had eaten once today. She was out of cigarettes, which was going to be a problem unless she made a concerted effort to give up smoking.

When she arrived at the hotel Jimmy was at the desk and waved her over. "I showed my watch to my classmates today and I can't tell you how impressed they were. They all want one just like it."

"I'm afraid that's the only one I have," Lauren said.

"That's what I told them—that they'd have to go all the way to Switzerland if they wanted to buy one."

"Can you tell me how much cigarettes are, Jimmy?"

"Ten cents. How much are they in Los Angeles?"

"I suppose they're the same. I've been out of the country for a while and I thought the price might've gone up." Lying was becoming second nature.

"Could I ask you a personal question?"

"Sure."

"Is that how women in Switzerland dress?"

Lauren smiled. "A few of them. The ones who ride horses a lot."

Jimmy was nodding. "I can see where it would be more practical. I'm afraid you're going to get a lot of stares in San Francisco dressed like that, though."

"I have already. I'm going to have to do some shopping for clothes while I'm here. I wonder, Jimmy, would you be interested in buying something else? I still haven't got my money changed and I need some cigarettes."

"I guess Swiss women smoke, too."

"All the women in Europe smoke," said Lauren, realizing she was singlehandedly ruining the reputations of
a continent of women.

"What was it you wanted to sell?"

Lauren reached into her purse for one of her ballpoint
pens and showed Jimmy how it worked. When he wanted
to understand the mechanism, she unscrewed it and
showed him the plastic container of ink. "When the ink
runs out, of course, it'll no longer work," she told him.

"I'd love to have that to show my class," he said, "but
I don't have much money to spare."

"If I could just get a pack of cigarettes..."

"Oh, I can do better than that." He reached under the
counter and brought up two packs, one opened but almost full, the other unopened. "Here, take these. And
I'll make sure there's a pack here for you every day for
the next week. How would that be?"

Lauren breathed a sigh of relief. Coping would be hard
enough without losing the help of her worst habit.
"Thanks, Jimmy—that's perfect. I wonder if I might ask
another favor of you?"

"Sure, Miss Hall—anything."

"It's a little dark in my room and I like to read."

"If you can wait until my break, I'll bring you up an
oil lamp."

She thanked him again and took the stairs to her room.
She hadn't thought the hotel would have maid service,
but when she got to her room her bed was made and her
belongings neatly arranged. She wondered what the maid
thought of her strange possessions.

She was sorry now that she had asked Early Cruz for help. He was a man, after all, and when were men ever any help when you needed them? In her own times she wouldn't have called on a male friend for help; it would be a female friend she would ask. Even in her own family, much as she loved her father, it was her mother she went to when she had a problem. In the first place, men always wanted something in return. And in the second, men rarely had any good advice to give, anyway.

Still, she had a feeling San Francisco in 1906 was a man's world. Well, she was damned if she was going to give in to that kind of old-fashioned thinking. She had a good brain and a healthy body, and there was no reason in the world she shouldn't survive.

It was the little things that were hard. The fact that she had no money or clothes, that her hair was too short, that she stood out in a crowd. She would have to wait for her hair to grow, but there *was* something she could do about clothes. She could steal them. She wasn't a dishonest person and she'd hate like hell to end up in jail, but surely the loss of a dress wouldn't make some woman destitute. And maybe a hat to cover her short hair. She could manage very well with her own underwear and her own boots.

Once she had a proper outfit, she was certain she would be able to find work. She was getting to be a pretty good liar and she could make up references in Southern California that they couldn't check. Or she could keep up the story about Switzerland. If the references were checked by mail it would take quite a while before her employer found out she was lying, and she'd work hard for them in the interim.

But once she was settled in a job that would pay for her room and board, the possibilities were endless. If she were smarter, she could be an inventor. Unfortunately, she didn't have the knowledge. She didn't know what made a television work or a radio. She wasn't even sure how hot water heaters worked; they would certainly add to the comfort of everyday living. But she could try to write all the books she had read and paint a few pictures that could pass for Picassos and sing some songs that would make them stand up and listen.

The possibilities really were endless! She could open a discotheque, or the first Kentucky Fried Chicken outlet, or start a clothing store for women with designs that would knock their eyes out.

Sure, she could do all that—and they would probably lock her up and throw away the key.

Well, she'd start small. She'd start with stealing herself some clothes. After all, she had a lot of years ahead of her to try to turn 1906 into 1987.

When the knock came at the door she figured it was Jimmy with the lamp, but when she opened it, Early was standing there.

"I want to talk to you," he said, his tone mournful.

"Come on in," she invited, stepping aside.

"That's not proper. I thought maybe—"

"I don't care if it's proper or not, Early. If you want to talk to me it's going to have to be here."

He walked past her into the room, his eyes grazing the writing on her T-shirt. She was wearing one of the Summer Games shirts she'd bought in L.A. several years earlier.

He sat down in the chair and she sat cross-legged on the bed, more at ease than he appeared to be. She wasn't worried at all about having Early alone with her in her room. She was reasonably sure that men in 1906 were gentlemen.

His eyes were looking everywhere but at her, and she broke the silence by asking, "Did you come to warn me you turned me in to the police?"

He shook his head, then abruptly got up and began pacing around the room. "Why in hell should I help you?" he finally began, but before she could answer, he went on, "You talk peculiar, you know that? You look peculiar, you have a peculiar name, you dress peculiar and you own some pretty peculiar things. You aren't like anyone I've ever known."

"I understand that," she said, trying to soothe him. "I apologize for bothering you today. It won't happen again, I promise. You can just forget you ever met me."

Her words didn't appear to placate him; he still looked agitated. "You know why I told you to get out of there today? You want to know why?"

"I guess I was bothering you."

"You were bothering me all right. And you know what was bothering me the most? I was starting to believe you!"

"I wasn't lying to you, Early."

He sank back down in the chair, his legs straight out in front of him and covering half the width of the room. "That's what I was afraid of."

"And I'm not crazy."

"That I'm not so sure of."

"Then what're you doing here if you think I'm crazy?"

"Damned if I know."

Lauren got off the bed and grabbed her duffel bag. She put it on the bed, unzipped it, and took out the hair dryer. "This is an electric hair dryer," she said, handing it to him, "and this is a book published in 1986—go on, open it up and see. And this is a pair of plastic sandals— I don't think plastic's been invented yet, has it? And here—this should be proof positive." She handed him a copy of *People* magazine.

His eyes widened as he looked at the picture of a current TV star wearing a bikini. "You giving me smut to look at?"

"That's not smut, Early. That's the way women dress for the beach where I come from."

One corner of his mouth turned up. "Maybe I live in the wrong times."

She sat back down on the bed. "I'm not asking for your help anymore, Mr. Cruz. I just don't want you to think I'm a nut, that's all."

He cocked one eyebrow at her. "A nut?"

"Crazy. A nut means crazy."

"One thing I'll admit to, Lauren Hall. You're sure the most interesting woman I've ever met."

"You mean I'm a freak."

"Sure you're a freak. I guess I'd be a freak if I suddenly showed up a few dozen years from now."

"Then you believe me?"

"I didn't say that. Tell me how you got here, or how you think you did."

She tried to tell him, but he kept interrupting. First it was about her driving her own car. He didn't seem surprised when she said that everyone drove, that there were no more horses and buggies.

"I figured they were on their way out," he said. "But women drive? Alone?"

"Why not? It might surprise you, Early, but women do just about everything men do in 1987."

"You don't have to stretch the story to get my attention."

She ignored his comment and continued. Next he wanted to know what a McDonald's was, and wasn't satisfied when she told him he was better off not knowing. When she got to the part about the earthquake, though, he kept nodding, and she thought that at least he believed that.

"And then you woke up and were back in time?"

She nodded. "I didn't know it at first. And then, even after I'd seen the evidence, I didn't really believe it. Like you, I didn't believe in time travel."

"But here you are."

"Yes, here I am."

"Well, you're either a damn good liar or you're telling the truth. In which case, you could be crazy or you could be sane."

"And what's your opinion?"

"I'm still thinking on it."

"I appreciate your listening to me, Early, but I've decided I don't need your help."

"You need it."

"No, I don't. I'm quite capable of taking care of my-self—"

"You're coming home with me."

That was the last thing she'd expected him to say. "No, Early—no way!"

"I'm not suggesting anything improper, so don't go getting your back up. I've got plenty of room in my house—"

"I said no. I'm not moving in with any man."

"You think I like the idea? Hell, I've been avoiding women like the plague my whole life, but it seems to me it'll solve your problems for the moment."

"I appreciate the offer, Early, particularly since you equate women with the plague, but I've been doing a lot of thinking and I'm pretty sure I can get a job."

"Doing what?" He looked skeptical.

"Housework."

He started to smile. "Well, if it's housework you have in mind, I could use a little of that myself."

"I have no intention of being your maid, Early."

"You're a stubborn woman, Lauren, you know that? There are plenty of women who'd be happy to be my maid."

"Then get one of them."

His smile disappeared. "I could turn you over to the authorities, you know."

"Blackmail now, Early?"

He got to his feet. "No. You don't have to worry about that, woman—I wouldn't turn you in. And I won't drag you over to my place by force, either, if you're worried about that."

"No. You don't seem to be the forceful kind."

"No?" He seemed a little insulted.

"No. And I do appreciate the offer, honest."

She climbed off the bed as he headed for the door. He stood there for a moment looking down at her. "Just a word of advice, Lauren. If I were you I wouldn't go tooting around town in that shirt you're wearing."

"I didn't plan on it. I do have some sense, you know."

"Well, stay out of trouble," he said, opening the door and walking out into the hall.

"I'll try," she replied, almost smiling at the thought of what he would say if he knew what she had planned for that night. He probably wouldn't look too kindly on her playing burglar in his fair city.

Chapter Three

Police Searching for Novice Burglars

SAN FRANCISCO, Jan. 3—A Leavenworth Street residence was robbed last night and the thieves passed up a valuable plate for minor articles of clothing. Police surmise that the burglars were not professionals.

NO MATTER HOW LAUREN ARRANGED the garments, she ended up looking ridiculous. The skirt was too short, which she didn't mind, but the waist was too small and she couldn't fasten it. The blouse was skimpy in the shoulders and large in the bust, which was the only place where the buttons would do up. And the fabric was so stiff, the high collar made her neck break out in a rash when she'd had the blouse on for only a minute. The other thing she'd managed to grab in the short time she was in the house was a man's suit coat. It fit, but was hardly practical.

If she'd just spent a few more minutes there and not panicked at the first noise she'd heard, she wouldn't have to go out tonight and try again. She hoped she would be more successful the second time, because if she had to go out a third time she'd give up. A life of crime wasn't as easy as it sounded.

Lauren left the hotel after dark, making her way to one of the neighborhoods that had houses with yards. She walked slowly along the streets, biding her time until she saw what she'd been waiting for, a couple leaving their house together. She figured she'd really lucked out since the two were women; one appeared to be middle-aged and the other her elderly mother. At least this time she wouldn't end up with a man's jacket by mistake.

She stood silently in the shadow of a tree until they'd turned a corner and were out of sight. Then she walked by the house a couple of times, checking for lights in any of the windows. The third time she approached she un-latched the front gate then closed it behind her. Circling the house on the grass, she searched for any signs that someone was still inside. But there were no lights, not even the flickering waver of candlelight from within.

She tried the back door but it was locked. Still, if none of the windows were open, she'd return to the door and knock out one of the panes of glass to gain entry. She didn't feel that she was hurting the women: the house looked expensive and she was certain the occupants would be able to afford to replace the glass and the items of clothing.

The third window she tried opened. She pushed it up as far as she could, then pulled herself up and over the windowsill, thankful for the strength in her arms, ac-quired by the weightlifting she'd done in another life.

She landed on top of a kitchen table, scattering the items covering it. She slid to the floor and pushed what felt like salt and pepper shakers and a napkin holder back to the center of the table. If possible, she wanted to de-lay the time before the owners of the house suspected the robbery, and that meant not leaving a mess behind her.

She lit her lighter and found the back stairs off the kitchen. In total darkness, she made her way slowly up the stairs, silent in her running shoes, then felt along the wall in the hallway until she came to a room. She entered and flicked her lighter again. It was a bedroom, and it boasted a large wardrobe against one wall.

She was running dangerously low on lighter fluid, but she wanted to do the job right this time and flicked the Bic again. When she opened the door to the wardrobe, she discovered several skirts and blouses inside. She drew out one of the skirts and was holding it to her waist to see if it would fit when a shaky voice called out, "Miz Roberts, that you?"

Lauren felt as if she were going to have a heart attack. Dropping the skirt to the floor, she stood in shocked silence. She'd miscalculated badly and someone was home after all.

"Miz Roberts, you in your room?" came the voice again, and Lauren moved quickly toward the hall. Three steps forward and she bumped into a large form that was blocking her way. Judging from the scent in the air, it was a woman and not a man.

Thinking quickly, Lauren flicked her lighter again and illuminated the woman's frightened face. When she saw the flame in front of her, the woman began to scream as though a flock of evil spirits were pursuing her. Lauren quickly squeezed past her and headed for the stairs. Still holding the lighter, she took the stairs two steps at a time and ran for the kitchen window.

Once outside she could still hear the screams, and it was obvious the neighbors could, too, because people were coming out of the houses nearby and looking in her direction. She tried to make a run for it, but halfway down the block a man grabbed her and wouldn't let go.

"Hold on, boy," she heard, "you aren't going nowhere."

"I FIGURED IT WAS YOU as soon as I heard about it." Early surveyed her through the bars of her cell, a cigarette dangling from his mouth.

Lauren remained seated on the wooden stool, afraid to look happy to see him until she knew why he'd come.

"Don't you want to hear how I knew?"

Lauren shrugged, wishing she had a cigarette.

He gave a chuckle. "It was the torch of fire that grew miraculously out of the devil's hand." The chuckle became a laugh, and soon he was choking on his cigarette smoke.

"Very funny," said Lauren.

He finally got himself under control. "Now you've got to admit that's funny. The police are still having a laugh over it. Everyone thought the poor woman was dreaming. Everyone but me. I, of course, had seen a torch of fire like that just the other night, so I wasn't laughing. What were you up to anyway, Lauren Hall, robbing two widow ladies?"

"I don't suppose you'd get me a lawyer," she said.

"You suppose right."

She gave him a baleful look. "What was I supposed to do, Early? My money's no good and I needed some clothes."

He was shaking his head. "The reasons people give for turning to a life of crime."

"If you came here to give me a sermon, Early, you can just leave. Anyway, I didn't get anything."

"True enough, but there was also unlawful breaking and entering."

"So I'm going to be locked up for life, is that it?"

Early grinned. "This isn't the dark ages, Lauren. You'll get a fair trial."

"And *then* be locked up for life."

"Maybe. I don't think the judge is going to take too kindly to a woman dressed like a man. Not all men can fully appreciate a sight like that."

She could have sworn his grin had turned to a leer. Still, he was outside and she was inside and that gave him the decided advantage. Lauren stood up and approached the bars. "Could I have a cigarette?"

"I don't know, Lauren—you seem to like setting fires."

"I wasn't setting fires, damn it, and you know it!"

"My, my. Is that how women in your day and age talk?"

"We talk a lot worse than that. I've been controlling myself up to now."

Looking thoroughly amused for no reason that she could discern, he handed his lit cigarette through to her. "That's a pretty bad habit you have."

"You should know," she said, taking a deep drag on the cigarette. She backed up, not wanting him to take it away from her.

"Thought about my offer anymore?"

"You mean to be your maid?"

"The very one."

"There's nothing to think about. I told you I didn't plan on being your maid."

Early's amusement was growing by leaps and bounds. He was fairly grinning when he said, "Of course job offers are going to just *pour* in while you're behind bars."

Her expression brightened. "Actually, being locked up might have solved my problem. At least I won't need money in here, and they're bound to feed me."

He started to turn away. "Well, if you change your mind, tell the sergeant you want to see me."

She sat down in dejection, sorry now she'd antagonized him. Talking to him was better than talking to herself. "Thanks for the offer again, Early, but I doubt I'll be free to take you up on it, even if I wanted to."

He turned back. "Let me make one thing clear, Lauren. If I vouch for you, I can get you out of here right now."

She practically leaped off the stool. "Well, why didn't you say so?"

"Because the condition is, you come home with me."

She stood there weighing the pros and cons. Except the cons turned out to be nonexistent. After all, there was nothing that said she couldn't quit her job as Early's maid the first hour she was there. And he'd look pretty silly bringing her back to the police station after all the lying he was going to have to do to get her out.

"All right," she agreed with a distinct look of politeness.

"I can see the prospect sure thrills you," said Early, and he put a key into the lock and opened the cell door.

"WHY WAS THAT so easy?" she asked him when they got out to the street. The policemen had even been polite to her.

"You mean getting you out?"

"You know what I mean."

"They were going to let you go anyway. The woman you scared described you as a tall man weighing at least 250 pounds. They're still out looking for him."

Lauren stopped walking. "Since you tricked me, Early Cruz, I feel no compunction about breaking our bargain."

He grabbed her arm forcibly and propelled her along the sidewalk. "What're you going to do otherwise, Lauren? Go out and rob some more houses?"

"You could've at least left me there until they fed me. I haven't eaten since that meal you bought me two days ago."

"You can cook dinner for us when we get to my place."

His place turned out to be a Victorian monstrosity on Powell, so big Lauren figured it must be a boarding-house. Suspecting a joke, she was surprised when they entered and she saw it was a one-family house.

"You live in this place alone?" she asked him.

"Just me."

"You're crazy, Early—no *way* am I going to clean a place this size."

"Just keep up the rooms we live in. I'm not an ogre, Lauren. I'm not going to inspect the premises for dirt every night."

"I've never seen such an ugly place," she pronounced once the lights were on and she surveyed the main room. It was wallpapered and filled with overstuffed, hideous furniture; every place a knickknack could reside, it did. "Don't you get claustrophobia in here?"

"Maybe, only I don't know what that means."

"I'll make you a deal, Early. You don't need a maid. What you need is an interior decorator. Why don't you pay me to fix this place up for you?"

"What's the matter with it? This was my parents' house. It's done up real fine."

"It's so...so out of date!"

"Not for 1906, it isn't."

She was too hungry to further the argument at the moment. "All right, Early, show me to the kitchen."

It was as unattractive as the rest of the place and looked as if it was never used. "Where's the refrigerator?"

"The what?"

"The icebox."

"On the back porch, but it's empty."

She glanced around. "No electrical appliances?"

"Just what you see. Any more questions?"

"Yeah, you got anything to eat in the house?"

He had the good sense to look a little sheepish. "I guess not. You're going to have to take care of the shopping. I generally eat out."

"If you don't feed me soon—"

He held up his hands in surrender. "Don't take a fit now, Lauren. What I thought we'd do is stop by the hotel for your things and get a meal there. I just wanted you to see your new home first, that's all."

"Some new home," Lauren muttered as he led her out of the house. She only hoped it had a bathroom.

OVER DINNER she experienced misgivings and second thoughts and tried to voice them to Early. He ignored them all, threatening her with everything but bodily harm if she didn't return with him to his house.

"Early, I can manage all right. All I need is a few clothes and I'll be able to get a job." She told him of her plan to use false references.

"You'll never get a job, Lauren. You're too different and the women aren't going to like it. And you don't act like a woman's supposed to act, which is going to make you instantly suspect."

"It's only for now—I have other ideas for later on."

"Fine, you can tell me about them later. Right now you need someone watching out for your interests, and I guess I got stuck with the job." He ordered them each a brandy, then passed her a cigarette. "I hope you know you're ruining my reputation. Being seen in San Francisco with a woman who smokes is no small thing."

"Yes, and I'll ruin it even more by moving in with you."

"No, you won't. I have it planned that you're my cousin's daughter who's come to keep house for me while she looks for a husband. It'll be believable—you wouldn't *credit* the number of women who come here for that very purpose."

"Just how old do you think I am, Early?"

"Twenty-one. Maybe twenty-two. Don't worry, not every girl is married by that age."

"Early, I'm thirty-one. Too old to be your innocent young cousin and too old for you to start acting fatherly with me. As for what you said before, I don't need anyone to look out for my interests. I can look out for them very well by myself."

"You can't be thirty-one."

"You saw my driver's license."

"No one looks like you at thirty-one. Hell, you could pass for a twelve-year-old boy if you cut your hair off and wore the right clothes."

"The only reason I don't look like thirty-one to you is because all the women of thirty-one you know have probably had a dozen kids."

"Not all of them," he said in a way that led her to believe he wasn't the misogynist he made himself out to be.

"Look, I've got my room for two weeks—"

"And no money to eat. What's the problem, Lauren? I'm trying to help you and you act like I'm out to do you wrong."

She decided to give in gracefully, or at least as gracefully as she could to a man. "Okay, Early, I'll give it a try. How much you going to pay me?"

"You're getting room and board—"

"I want a salary, too. There're things I need and I don't want to have to sell off everything I have to get them."

He reached into his pocket for his toothpick and settled it between his teeth. "Five dollars suit you?"

"Five dollars?"

"Those're good wages with room and board thrown in. I'll even throw in some clothes."

"Big deal."

"No, I mean it. I still have all of my mother's clothes around somewhere. They might be a little out of date, but I don't reckon you'll know the difference."

She was about to say something about that when she saw the light in his eyes and realized he was joking. "How much do you make working for the *Chronicle*?" she asked him.

"Sixty-five."

"A week?"

The corner of his mouth turned up. "A month, and it's good wages, too."

"Does that mean my five dollars would be for a whole *month*?"

"Five dollars goes a long way."

She settled back in her chair. "All right, Early. I guess that sounds fair enough." She thought of telling him how much she made at her job as a systems analyst, but it didn't seem fair. Anyway, he was probably right about five dollars going a long way. And if she used her wits, she was sure she could think of ways to augment that income.

"Ready to go home?" he asked her.

"As ready as I'll ever be," she replied.

"Come on, Lauren—if *I* can put a good face on it, surely *you* can."

She realized she was behaving like a spoiled child when all he was trying to do was help her. She should be happy for any help she could get. She managed a smile. "You're a good man, Early Cruz. Even if—"

He held up his hand to silence her. "Now don't go spoiling the first nice words you've had to say about me."

"Just don't hold your breath till the next time."

"If I did that, I'd probably be dead."

"Exactly," she said, deducing it was the first time he'd heard the expression. Sometimes, she thought wryly, talking to Early was like trying to be understood in a foreign language.

Chapter Four

Gas and Electric Appliance Exhibit

You are invited to visit the new Gas and Electric Exhibition Car at the corner of Van Ness Avenue and Sutter Street, opposite St. Dunstan's. Full display and demonstrations of Gas Ranges, Water Heaters, Grates and many novel and wonderful electric appliances, including Electric Instantaneous Water Heaters, Chafing Dishes, X-Ray Machinery, Doctors' and Dentists' Outfits. Courteous explanation of all appliances and demonstrations of Cooking Cheaply by Gas.

The Gas Company

LAUREN SLEPT LATE. When she woke, it was quiet in the house and she supposed Early had gone to work. He'd given her money the night before to shop for food, then shown her to his parents' room on the second floor.

"No one's used it since my mother died last year," he told her, watching as she looked around the large room. She was sure the decor was considered the height of luxury, but to her the room seemed dark and gloomy and gave off an odor of mustiness.

Still, she'd slept well, even if the mattress was too soft. She got up and went down the hall to the one bathroom in the house. It had the usual cold running water, which Early had pointed out to her with pride, and a toilet that, when you pulled a chain, flushed loud enough to shake the house. A cloudy mirror hung over the marble washbasin and she studied her pale reflection. What she needed was either a tan or some makeup. And she wasn't going to get a tan in San Francisco in January or make-up—as she knew it—in 1906. She was loath to use the makeup she had because she knew it would soon be gone.

Her brown hair, which was normally curly, hung limp against her head. She couldn't remember when she'd last washed it, but today she would boil some water and try to get it clean. Her hair and the rest of her. She couldn't tell with herself but she had a feeling she was beginning to smell like the rest of the people she'd come in contact with. Most of her clothes were dirty, too.

She'd already seen the first floor, which had a living room (called a parlor by Early), dining room, kitchen and pantry. She now explored the second floor. Besides the bedroom she'd slept in and a smaller one used by Early, there were three more rooms. One had what looked like a sewing machine set up in one corner and little else, one was another bedroom and the third was the coziest room she'd seen yet, with a rolltop desk, swivel chair and several bookcases filled with books.

Lauren wasn't much of a reader, but she figured with no television or movies, books were going to be the only entertainment going. She glanced at the titles but found nothing of interest. They were all leatherbound and dusty and had small print. And she didn't find any that were novels except for a couple of Dickenses, and 1906 San Francisco was bad enough without reading about Dickens's London.

She decided to explore further and went up the narrow stairway leading to the third floor. There she got a pleasant surprise. She discovered a warren of small rooms. The ceilings were lower than those in the rest of the house, plaster walls hadn't been papered but were left unfinished. Even though the windows were as dirty as the rest of the windows in the house, the rooms seemed brighter without the heavy layers of draperies and dark walls. If it was all right with Early, she'd move a bed up there for herself and fix the place up. With a little ingenuity, she might be able to make it resemble the apartment she'd had.

Back in the kitchen, she lit the stove the way Early had shown her, then found a pot and put some water on to boil. She washed her hair in cold water, then, when the water boiled, rinsed it well with warm. Opening the door to the stove, she sat in front of it and brushed her hair until it dried. It was a lengthy process, but if everyone else in San Francisco managed—and the women she'd seen had very long hair—then she supposed she could manage, too.

There were three very large wardrobes in the bedroom she was using and she searched through them for clothes to wear. All three were filled with women's clothing but Early had neglected to tell her that his mother had been a very large woman. The skirts she tried on fell right down to the floor over her slim hips, and the blouses were large enough for her to wear as roomy night shirts. There were a few dresses in heavy, dark material. She tried one on, and with the help of her belt around the waist and by blousing the top of the dress, she thought she might be able to "pass" in the streets—especially with one of the women's capes worn over it.

She began to get into the spirit of dressing up. It reminded her of when she'd been a little girl and her mother had let her dress in her clothes. Lauren sat down on the floor to try on some of the shoes. They were rather tight, but not as uncomfortable as she'd thought they'd be. In fact they weren't so different from some of the lace-up boots she'd worn in the past. The hats looked comical, but they made her short hair appear a little more appropriate.

Feeling as though she were outfitted for a costume party, Lauren put the money Early had left her in one of the pockets of the dress and went off to find a grocery store.

Shopping was a debacle. There was no one store that carried everything. There was a butcher shop whose hanging animals, barely dead it seemed, made her gag, and she quickly left. Another store was stocked with jars and boxes of packaged foods and spices, but she couldn't tell one from another, and when she found herself being eyed by both customers and clerks, she fled back to the street. The smells from a bakery beckoned her, and she arrived home with only one purchase—a large loaf of freshly baked bread.

She had consumed half the loaf by the time Early came home from work that evening.

She'd dusted the parlor and brought in wood for the fireplace, which she'd managed to get going without much trouble. Eschewing the overhead light, which was dim at best, she had rounded up most of the oil lamps and set them around the room so that it didn't seem quite as depressing as before. She had also gathered up almost

all the figurines that had resided on the numerous tables
and put them safely away in the pantry. On a small table
she had placed in front of a velvet loveseat, she had a
bottle of brandy and two glasses ready and waiting. She
had a feeling she was behaving more like a wife than a
maid, but she didn't feel like a maid. Not that she felt like
a wife. She thought their arrangement might turn out to
be more like roommates than anything else. At least she
hoped so.

"Did you manage all right?" were his first words to
her, his sharp eyes taking in the jumpsuit she was wearing.

"Not very well, I'm afraid."

He sat down in one of the chairs and looked at the
brandy bottle. "A drink before dinner?"

"I had a little trouble shopping for food, Early."

"Oh? What kind of trouble?" He sounded as though
he thought it wouldn't be serious.

"I couldn't tell what anything was. And the butcher
shop—it made me sick."

He reached for the bottle and poured them each a
drink, suddenly looking as though he could use one.
"What *did* you manage to get?"

"A loaf of bread. And I've eaten most of it."

He was nodding his head and she could see it took a
real effort on his part not to laugh. "And here I thought
I was going to get a home-cooked meal tonight."

"If you could do the grocery shopping..."

He shook his head. "It seems to me that's what I'm
paying you to do. However, I'll stop home tomorrow at
lunchtime and take you to the stores the first time. It

might be easier if I set up accounts for you there while I'm at it."

"Thank you, Early."

"And get that humble expression off your face—I don't recognize you when you look like that."

Lauren laughed and reached for her drink. "Another thing, Early—you didn't tell me your mother was about twice my size."

"There's a sewing machine upstairs. I figured you could take her clothes in to fit you."

"I don't know how to sew. Do you?"

"Me? Of course not. Find a dressmaker, then, and get fixed up." He gave a pointed look at her jumpsuit. "I'm not going to continue being seen with you in public in things like that."

"And I'm not going to wear dresses that hang clear down to the ground!"

He must have noticed her mutinous expression, because he smiled and said, "All right, a compromise. I don't care how you dress around the house, but at least put a long cape over your clothes when we go out in public. I've already put out the word that you're a relative from the East who's going to keep house for me, so don't put me to shame, Lauren."

She gave in and nodded. Anyway, she didn't like being stared at any more than he liked her to be. "I have a favor to ask, Early."

He grunted.

"I'd like to live on the third floor if that's all right with you."

"That's just maids' rooms up there. And since my parents' maids always lived out, the rooms aren't even finished."

"I know. I like them better that way. Would you have any objections to my fixing them up a little and having my room up there?"

"Is this going to cost me money?"

"Not much. All I need right off is some white paint."

"White paint? What do you want white paint for?"

"You'll see. Could I have some?"

He sighed. "There's all the white paint you could ever need out in the shed in back. I was going to have the house painted but never got around to it."

"Thanks, Early."

"You don't have to keep thanking me. It's bound to be interesting to see what you come up with."

FOR THE NEXT TWO WEEKS Lauren worked harder than she'd ever worked in her life. She cleaned the house more thoroughly than it had been cleaned since his mother died. After instructions from Early, she'd taken all the oriental rugs out to the backyard and hit them with a stick until the dust flew out. Then, on hands and knees, she scrubbed the floors. She also washed all the windows, but since it rained right after she'd done them, they became streaky.

It took a week to clean the house to her satisfaction, and then she started on the third floor. She chose the largest two rooms to live in and painted them white, cursing the fact that she had to use a brush and not a roller, which hadn't been invented yet, according to Early.

In the basement, which she'd investigated despite the presence of mice, she found some lovely wicker furniture that Early told her was used on the front porch in the summer. She dragged a settee, two chairs and two small tables upstairs and gave them a fresh coat of white paint. The flowered cushions were worn and stained, so she covered them with white linen sheets she'd found stacked in a cupboard in the hall. She still didn't know how to use the sewing machine and wasn't interested in learning, but she managed to cover the cushions by hand with a needle and thread. If you didn't look too closely at the stitches they looked pretty good.

There was no electricity on the third floor so she carried up several china oil lamps and covered the hand-painted flowers that decorated them with more white paint. She left the windows uncovered. The houses on either side of Early's were only two stories high, and she didn't much care if anyone looked in, anyway.

Instead or moving a bed upstairs, she dragged up the mattress only. She placed it on the floor in the corner of one of the rooms and arranged all the wicker furniture in the other. It was spartan, she needed some touches of color, but all in all it felt far more pleasant to her than the rest of the house.

She scoured the house for accessories but didn't come up with much. She didn't like any of the dark oil paintings on the walls with their ornate, gold leaf frames. She found a couple of plain blue saucers among the more formal dinnerware and used them as ashtrays. In the bottom cupboard of the pantry she discovered a large yellow pitcher and matching bowl, which she carried upstairs. When the flowers started to bloom in the spring she'd fill the pitcher with them.

She needed a wardrobe and dresser in her bedroom but couldn't carry them up by herself, so at the end of the second week she asked Early for his help.

"You're really going to live up there?" he queried.

"I'm already living up there. Want to see what I've done?"

He followed her up the stairs and she was disappointed when he pronounced her sitting room plain. She had been sure a man would prefer the less fussy atmosphere she had created.

"Don't you want anything on the floors?"

"Not unless you have something besides oriental rugs," she said.

"Aren't you going to cover the windows?"

"No, Early, I'm not. I happen to like sunlight in the rooms."

"Sunlight will ruin the rugs."

"But I don't have any rugs to *ruin*." At first she'd thought her sarcasm would go over his head, but she'd learned that he could be just as sarcastic when it pleased him.

His eyes almost popped out when he saw the mattress on the floor. "How'd you get that up here by yourself?"

"I carried it. I'm not weak, you know."

"I suppose you're too weak to carry the bed up, though, am I right?"

"I don't want a bed—I'm sleeping on the mattress."

"There are probably mice up here. You want mice running around your bed?"

She sighed. "Early, I'd rather share my bed with mice than have a bad back. The floor at least gives the mattress some support."

"Are you telling me people don't sleep in beds in the 1980s?"

"Look, Early, forget about the bed. But I do have a favor to ask."

Despite his obvious sufferance, he helped her carry a wardrobe and dresser upstairs that night, and the next day she painted them.

When her rooms were finished she found that she liked them very much but had nothing to do in them. She'd worn her Sony Walkman around the house the first week when she'd been cleaning, and the batteries had finally worn out. She kept thinking how great it would be if she had a TV set or even a radio, but knew such thoughts were a waste of time.

What she needed was a job. Or if not a job, at least a hobby. She knew it would be a good idea if she tried to learn to cook or sew, but neither interested her. Her cooking ran to various kinds of omelets, and after the first half dozen, Early began taking her out to dinner at night.

With no major project until spring, when she was going to plant a garden, she started going a little crazy around the house during the day. The nights were fine, since she had Early to talk to most of the time. Tuesday and Thursday nights he didn't come home until late, but she didn't ask him where he'd been. The other nights, though, they would sit in the parlor and smoke and drink brandy, and Lauren would tell him about the time she came from.

She told him about movies and television and pro football and what she knew of the two world wars—anything she could think of. He would interject questions and be seemingly fascinated, but when she asked him if he really believed all she was telling him, he shook his head.

"I'm not calling you a liar, Lauren, and it's sure interesting to listen to, but . . ."

"But you don't believe it."

He grinned. "Well, if I live long enough to see any of it, then I'll believe you all right."

"Well," she countered, "I think the First World War is just a few years off, so you'll believe me then."

"When's it supposed to start?"

"I don't remember."

Early looked doubtful. "A big event like the whole world at war and you can't *remember*?"

"Early, it was something I learned in school. Do you remember the year the Civil War started?"

"Of course I do!"

Lauren sighed. "Well, for all I know you fought in it."

That ended the discussion that night.

She decided to take up painting as a hobby, and one Saturday afternoon when he came home earlier than usual, she got him to take her to a store that sold art supplies. She was amazed at how many paints and canvasses and brushes she was able to purchase for five dollars, and when she got them home she set them all out in one of the empty rooms on the third floor.

That Monday she started in on her career as an artist. She couldn't draw very well and didn't know the first thing about painting, but it didn't take her long to cover several of the canvasses with the kind of pictures she'd seen in galleries all over town. In the 1980s, that was. She hung them on the walls with nails and that night dragged Early upstairs to view them.

"What're they supposed to be?" he asked her.

"They're not supposed to be anything—they're modern art."

"A child could've done them."

"That's what people said about Picasso." Which then meant she had to explain all about Picasso to him. "I think he's probably alive and in Paris about now," she told him.

But all he said was, "Well, I've never heard of him, and if he paints like *that*, I don't expect I ever will."

THE FIRST TIME Lauren started thinking of Early in any kind of personal way occurred on the second Sunday she was living with him. They'd just had an omelet and were sitting around the kitchen reading the Sunday paper when he said, "How about boiling me some water for a bath?"

She almost sighed out loud in relief that the man was finally going to bathe. She wouldn't say his smell was exactly rank, but it came quite close.

She immediately got up and put four pots of water on to boil, then turned to him and said, "Can I ask you a personal question, Early?"

"You're going to anyway."

"I just wondered, don't you ever wear casual clothes?"

"What're you talking about?"

"Well, you can't be comfortable sitting around all the time in a suit and tie."

"What am I *supposed* to wear with you around the house?"

"What'd you wear before I moved in?"

"I used to take my jacket and tie off at night."

"But you kept on the rest?"

"I know you did things different in 1987, Lauren—God knows you've told me as much enough times—but I happen to be from a more civilized time, and we don't go around half naked the way you seem to like to do."

Lauren was amazed. She'd thought she'd been particularly modest since she'd lived there. "Wouldn't you rather be more comfortable?"

"What do you suggest, I put on that leapsuit of yours?"

"You know what it's called, Early."

"Leapsuit, jumpsuit, what's the difference?"

She didn't continue the argument, but when he was in the bath she got her gray sweatshirt out of her wardrobe, the only one that didn't have any writing on it, and took it downstairs.

"You dressed yet?" she kept calling out to him, and when he finally said he was, she opened the door to the bathroom just in time to see him putting on his suit jacket again.

She held the sweatshirt out to him. "Why don't you try this, Early?"

"You trying to dress me in women's clothes?"

"Men wear them, too. Everyone wears them. Come on, take off that jacket and shirt and try it. It's not going to kill you, and if you don't think it's comfortable you can take it off."

He looked extremely dubious, but he took it from her, then just stood there.

"Well, go on."

"Would you mind leaving the room, Lauren?"

"Oh, come on, Early—I've seen men's chests before."

For the first time she got a real rise out of him. "*What* did you say?"

"You heard me, Early."

"I don't know what kind of woman you are, Lauren, but I guess I was mistaken about you."

"Are you telling me no woman's ever seen your chest?"

The man was actually turning red, and it was all Lauren could do to keep from laughing at him.

"*You're* not going to see it" was all he said.

She stomped out of the bathroom, gave him about sixty seconds to change, then walked back in. He was pulling the sweatshirt over his head, giving her a clear look at his smooth, brown chest. Before he could see her, she backed out of the bathroom, then called out, "Here I come," before entering again.

And suddenly, for the very first time, she was seeing him as a man. The sight of his chest had jolted her a little, but then the sight of any man's chest after a period of abstinence might have done the same. What made her catch her breath was the way he looked in the sweatshirt. He had never seemed quite real to her in his three-piece suits. They made him look too old-fashioned, too much of an anachronism. But Early's lean dark face coming out the top of an ordinary sweatshirt was something else. She suddenly realized that if she could get him into some jeans and running shoes, he'd have the kind of looks she had been partial to in the old days. The old days being 1987 and thereabouts.

"What's the matter? Why're you staring at me like that?"

"It looks good on you, Early."

"It feels too soft—makes me uncomfortable."

"Because it's too *soft*? Come on, Early, give it a fair chance. No one's going to see you but me."

He was moving his shoulders around underneath the material, but at least he hadn't pulled the shirt off. "Maybe I'll wear it on Sundays. Just around the house."

"You should get a pair of Levi's to go with it."

"You mean like the ranchers wear?"

She nodded.

"They don't look comfortable to me."

"They are after you wear them a bit."

He refused to say anything more about it, but later she caught him stealing glances at himself in the mirror.

And more often than not, she found herself stealing looks at him.

THE ONE THING she did read each day was the *Chronicle*. Every part of it delighted her, from the news, which read like a history book, to the personals, which made her laugh. The idea came to her one day for no reason at all, and she couldn't wait for Early to get home that night to tell him about it. She even cooked him dinner—a roast chicken that was definitely overdone—so that they could discuss it at length and in privacy.

She'd convinced him the first week that eating in the dining room made no sense at all. When he said the kitchen table was for maids, she told him that since *she* was a maid, that's where she was eating, and he was welcome to join her if he wanted. After that they ate in the kitchen.

The night in question she set the table in the dining room for two reasons. One, the chairs were padded, and she had a feeling they'd be sitting in them for quite a while, and two, she wanted to put him in a good mood right off.

Instead of improving his mood, though, she managed to make him suspicious.

"What're you up to, Lauren?" he asked as soon as he saw the food on the dining room table.

"I fixed you such a nice dinner tonight I thought we could eat it in here."

"That was my second question. What made you cook dinner?"

"Nothing *made* me, Early, but I figured I could handle something as simple as a chicken and baked potatoes."

He seemed somewhat mollified as he sat down at the head of the table. He was even nice enough not to mention how tough the chicken was, but he really went after it with his knife.

"I have a favor to ask of you, Early," she said when dinner was finished and they were drinking coffee—his regular, hers watered down.

"I should've known it."

"It's no big deal. It's just that I've lived off you long enough and I think I should get a job."

"You unhappy here, Lauren?"

"Most of the time."

"Look, if this is too much for you, we can hire a maid."

She choked on the coffee. "Do you hear what you're saying, Early? *I'm* the maid. Why would you *hire* a maid to *help* a maid?"

He shrugged. "A house this size usually has more help."

"It's not the housework, Early. I haven't minded that. At least not too much. But I'm bored. I can do everything that needs to be done around here in a couple of hours, and the rest of the day I have nothing to do."

"Maybe you could get someone to teach you to use that sewing machine."

"The *hell* with the sewing machine. Even if I learned to sew, I can't spend all my time making clothes."

"Most housewives are happy."

"Well, that's a stupid remark. First of all, I'm not a housewife. Maybe if I were, maybe if I had a bunch of children, I wouldn't be bored, but I sincerely doubt it. And I doubt whether you'd find most housewives are happy, either."

"What do you want from me, Lauren?"

"An introduction to your boss."

Now it was Early's turn to choke. "You want *what*?"

"You heard me right."

"You fancy yourself a newspaper reporter now? Or maybe you know how to set type, is that it?"

"Early, I've been reading that newspaper of yours every day. And it's a good paper, I like it. But there are a couple of columns it doesn't have that it could really use. But if you don't want to help me, Early, I can always go to one of the other papers with my ideas."

"I didn't know you were a writer."

"I'm not, but I can do the kind of writing I'm talking about."

"Okay, let's hear your ideas," he said, but she could tell he was only humoring her.

"My first idea was for an astrological column. Most of the newspapers in my day have them, and they're very successful."

"You mean like fortune telling?"

"I mean it gives advice each day according to astrological signs. And don't tell me that stuff isn't popular, because you've got people advertising in the classified section of the *Chronicle* under spiritualism, astrology and palmistry."

"Some people like that kind of thing."

"A lot of people must or they wouldn't keep advertising."

"Is that what you are? An astrologer?"

"No, but I bet I could be if I read a few books on it."

"Yes, well you obviously don't know my boss. That's the first question he'd ask you, and when you said that, he'd just get himself a *real* astrologer to do it. That is, if he liked the suggestion."

She smiled, ready to hit him with her best idea. She'd only thrown in the first one so he'd be more receptive to the second. "Let me tell you about 'Dear Abby,' Early."

Five minutes later he was beaten. "All right, all right, I'll set up an appointment for you. But after that you're on your own."

"Thank you, Early."

"'Dear Abby,' huh?"

"Well, I thought I'd call mine 'Dear Lauren.' And speaking of names, Early, can I ask you a personal question?"

"That's about all you ever *do* ask me."

"On the contrary, I censor what I say to you very thoroughly. But what I'd like to know is, how'd you get a name like Early Cruz?"

"Finally got around to asking me that, did you?"

"Well, it is a strange name."

"I was named for my grandfather who was a Methodist preacher back east."

"And the Cruz part?"

"That was my other grandfather—his family had one of the first Spanish land grants in California. It was De La Cruz, but my father shortened it."

"Thank you for telling me, Early."

He grinned. "Anything else you want to know?"

"No, that's all."

For some reason he seemed disappointed. As a reporter, he usually asked all the questions; maybe he liked being the one questioned for once. But that didn't sound like Early. He wasn't one to talk much about himself.

Chapter Five

Advice from Lauren

Dear Lauren, What do you think of a husband who doesn't allow his wife to go anywhere unaccompanied? On even a short journey to the milliner, my husband insists that either he accompanies me or one of the maids. I had more freedom than this before I was married. What would you suggest I do? A.K.

Dear A.K., Divorce him!

"DAMN IT, Lauren—" The editor ran his hands through his hair in a nervous gesture. "Sorry, pardon the language. But just what in *hell* is the meaning of this?"

"The meaning of what, H.H.?" Lauren made a move to swing one leg over the other, then realized she was wearing a dress and kept both legs in place on the floor.

"You know damn well—" He raised his fist to pound the desk, but stopped just a fraction of an inch from its surface. "I apologize again and assure you I don't normally lose my temper with ladies. But what the devil were you thinking of when you advised that woman to divorce her husband?"

She shrugged, not giving Henry Hawkins the satisfaction of unnerving her. "I thought it was good advice."

"It was *damnable* advice!" He swung around in his chair and appeared to be staring out the window for some kind of help. Finally he mumbled, "Sorry again."

"And you can quit apologizing for your language, H.H. I'm not going to curl up and die if I hear a swear word."

"If you were a *lady* you would!"

Lauren laughed. "Are you saying I'm not a lady?"

Henry Hawkins swung his chair back around and glared at her. "Don't think you have me fooled, miss. You haven't fooled me for one minute."

Lauren wondered what Early could have told him. The plan had been that Hawkins, the managing editor of the paper, wasn't to be let in on the secret. "No one gets anything past *you*, H.H."

"Damn right they don't, pardon the language. I've seen you sneaking cigarettes in the hall. I've heard tell that Early lets you dress in his clothes and sneaks you into bars. And if I didn't have such a high regard for Early, I'd have called you in on it, don't think I wouldn't. But I figure if Early can tolerate your unladylike behavior, well . . . live and let live, I always say."

Lauren got to her feet. "Thanks for your vote of confidence, sir. Now, if there's nothing else—"

"Sit down!"

Lauren complied.

"You're to blame, Lauren, if the divorce rate in San Francisco goes up. You know that, don't you?"

"I don't—"

"Shut up and listen to me! That's the third woman in a week you've told to get a divorce. You're putting ideas in these women's heads, Lauren, and no good's going to come of it."

"I happen to think you're wrong—"

"I'm not finished! You've got my wife—*my wife*—telling me what she can do these days. And when I say *no*, she quotes *you*!"

"H.H., we're getting hundreds of letters a day. Early says the circulation has gone up since—"

"Early said *what*? Early has no right talking circulation with you."

"I'm an employee, too," Lauren protested.

"At the moment that employment's *very* tenuous. Very tenuous indeed."

She figured since he knew already, what the hell, and she went ahead and got out her cigarettes. He noticed, but before he could say anything, she said, "You don't like it, H.H.? Fine. I'll take my column to the *Examiner*."

"Need a light?" asked Henry in a conciliatory voice, reaching out with a match. "No one's asking you to leave, Lauren. I'm only asking you to use a little restraint. I'm sure you'll agree with me that there are solutions to marital difficulties other than divorce."

"Maybe, but that's the fastest and the most effective."

"Lauren, who are you to talk? You've never even *experienced* the joys of married life."

"And I never will until women have a few more rights."

"I'm not getting in *that* argument with you again, so quit trying to bait me. All I'm asking you to do is be a little original. You call yourself a writer, well, learn how to write some word other than *divorce* all the time. Furthermore, your column might be getting that much mail, but we're also receiving a lot of complaints about some of your advice. And I think you know what I'm talking about."

"That's called controversy, Henry, and it helps to sell papers."

"It could help to get our building burned down some night, too, by an irate husband whose wife is spouting your advice to him."

"All right, Henry."

"All right?"

"That's what I said. Okay, no more divorce."

Henry's eyes narrowed and his face took on its sleeping cat expression. His bushy side whiskers added to the effect. "Why're you being so agreeable all of a sudden? I don't trust you when you're agreeable."

"I think you're right, I have been overdoing the divorce advice. I'm going to start telling the women to get an education so they can support themselves. Money is power, Henry, and the men have all the money."

His face flushed the colors of a sunset. "Lauren?"

"Yes, Henry?"

"Get the *hell* out of my office!"

"NEW DRESS?" asked Early when she stopped by his desk.

"I was getting tired of your mother's clothes. How does it look?"

"Skimpy—but an improvement."

"It only looks skimpy because I'm not wearing petticoats under it," she started to explain, then stopped when she saw she was embarrassing him. Early was easily embarrassed.

"Yes, well you look quite passable. Now if only your hair . . ."

"It'll grow, Early." Which was true, of course, but she had no intention of letting it grow long.

"What was Henry Hawkins yelling about?"

"You could hear?"

"The whole *building* could hear."

"He wants me to knock off advising women to divorce their husbands."

"I told you not to use that."

"Do I tell *you* how to write your stories, Early?"

"Don't get your back up with me. It was just a warning, that's all. But let me tell you, you're not endearing yourself to any of the married men around here with that kind of advice."

"Maybe, but their wives probably appreciate it."

He gave a sigh that spoke of long suffering, then asked, "You want to have lunch?"

"No, thanks, Early, not today. I have a huge stack of mail to get through. But if you bring some beer home, I'll cook you dinner tonight."

"Chicken?"

She nodded.

"I think we ought to eat out."

HER SHOULDER BAG stuffed with mail, Lauren headed out of the Chronicle Building. She stopped by there every day to pick up the mail, but she'd been hired with the stipulation that she work at home. Henry Hawkins hadn't thought it would do anything for the morale of the men to see a woman in a newspaper office, and that was fine with her. She'd fixed a third room in the attic into an office for herself, and it was a lot more pleasant than the Chronicle Building, with the added attraction that she could wear her own clothes when she worked.

She couldn't say she was happy. She didn't think she'd ever be happy living in 1906. But since getting the job she was at least more content. Writing her column filled up the hours between housework and shopping and took her mind off all the "what ifs" that went through her head whenever she thought back to the earthquake.

It also enabled her to save some money. H.H., being as cheap as he was prone to profanity, only paid her $15 a month, which had seemed a lot to her before she saw how popular her column had become. But the money Early paid her took care of cigarettes and other smaller items she might need, so she was banking the salary for the day she'd want to move out on her own.

She was amazed that day hadn't arrived yet. Surprisingly enough, she and Early got on well together, and the size of the house afforded them each privacy. She'd met most of Early's friends and assessed them with a discerning eye, coming quickly to the conclusion that he was the best of the bunch. She'd been truly fortunate in meeting him when she had, and she felt very much in his debt for all his help. In fact she hated to think what might have happened to her if she hadn't met Early when she did.

They still spent a lot of time talking in the evenings, but she had also learned what a gamester he was. One night he'd let it drop that when he went out on Tuesday and Thursday evenings, he went to a club where he played poker with his friends.

"And here I thought you had a lady friend," Lauren had teased him.

She didn't manage to embarrass him that time. "If I had a lady friend, I'd stay the night," he told her.

"In 1906?" she exclaimed, having thought the times were more "Victorian" than that.

"There're widow ladies around," he commented, but refused to discuss the subject any further.

Once she learned he liked cards, she insisted he play with her a couple of times a week. And the cards led to chess, and from then on their conversations usually took place during a game of some kind. He still had a somewhat condescending attitude when he played against her, but she was sure that with time he'd come around to regarding her as one of the boys.

Lauren spent the rest of the afternoon reading the mail that had come in and making notes on the letters. Only a small portion of the letters received would be printed in the newspaper, but Lauren had taken to answering some of the others personally. Not all of them, because many had problems similar to the ones being answered in the paper, but some of the letters were so private, and so sad, that she felt they deserved a reply.

She was learning more about women in 1906 from reading those letters than she ever would have by reading history books. So many of the women felt trapped, but unlike their counterparts in the 1980s, these women didn't have many options open to them. It wasn't plausible to think that droves of women would take her advice and divorce their husbands, because if they did they'd be destitute. Nor was the advice to get a college education going to be of much value, because the universities had such small quotas for women. Still, if she got enough women demanding to go to college, maybe the quotas would have to be increased.

Not all of the letters she received were from women. About twenty percent came from men. These were harder for her to answer, since they usually pertained to the writer's job, and most of the men were overworked and underpaid.

When she started the column it was with the intention of making it humorous, much in the manner of "Dear Abby," whom she was plagiarizing with no compunction. But the majority of the letters she received didn't call for humor, and she began to take her work seriously. On occasion, though, she did find herself chuckling when she thought how lucky these women were to get advice from someone with the experience of the ages, so to speak.

When Henry Hawkins had first hired her, the column was going to be printed only on Sundays, when the paper had a women's section. But the response had been so quick and so favorable, he'd gruffly informed her that she was going to have to do it every day of the week for the same salary. At the time she'd let him get away with this, because she was still somewhat in awe of him, but now that she thought she had his number, she was planning on hitting him for a raise soon.

When she finished going through the mail, making separate piles for the letters to answer, those to print and those to ignore, it was almost time for Early to be home, so she took a shower.

By means of a length of hose she'd had him get for her, she'd rigged up a shower over the tub. Granted, it still wasn't hot, but she found she could stand taking a cold shower better than a cold bath or carrying pots of hot water upstairs every time she wanted to bathe.

Early thought she was crazy for bathing so often, but her deodorant had run out and she wasn't about to start smelling like everyone else. Early still stuck to his weekly bath, but she couldn't help hearing him using the shower on occasion, though he never openly admitted to it.

She was dressed in her jeans and T-shirt when he got home, hoping he'd take her to one of the bars that served food and where she was already known as a boy.

Early was looking smug about something, then he reached into his pocket and held up an envelope. "I've got a surprise for you," he said.

"My severance pay?"

He was grinning now. "Nope, a good surprise."

"Is this going to be a guessing game, Early?"

"I've got two free tickets to the theater. Thought you might like to go."

"What're we seeing?"

"Something called *A Stranger in a Strange Land*."

"Sounds like me," said Lauren.

"I figured you'd say that."

"Maybe I ought to write a play about my experience."

"You're getting a strange enough reputation without that," remarked Early.

She put her new dress back on, and in honor of the occasion Early took her for dinner to the St. Francis, which had one of the fanciest restaurants in town.

For the first time Lauren began to appreciate the way women dressed in 1906. Up to now she'd seen only the dark clothes women wore in the business district. But tonight she noticed how lovely the women could look in the Gibson Girl style when the material was not dark serge.

She had thought the high necklines denoted the modesty of the times, but these evening dresses were often low cut and extremely becoming. She felt out of place in the plain dress she had bought to wear to the *Chronicle*.

When Early ordered champagne with their dinner she gave him a suspicious look. "What's the occasion, Early?"

"It'll just look better than you guzzling down beer."

"You're sure you're not working up to popping the question or something along those lines?"

"You mean *marriage*?" Early sounded horrified.

She relaxed at his expression. "Just checking. I thought maybe you figured you'd save money by marrying me."

"Well, it had occurred to me that since you're now getting a salary from the paper—"

"Forget it, Early! I earn that five dollars and you know it. If you want me to move out, say so, but unless you feel like cleaning that house and doing the shopping . . ."

"Don't get the idea you can intimidate me the way you do Henry Hawkins, Lauren. I got along fine before you moved in and I'll get along fine when it suits you to move out. As for the five dollars, there are a lot of girls in the city who'd be delighted to have room and board and a salary like that in exchange for so little work. And don't start telling me how you work yourself to death, either, because I know better.''

"You getting tired of me, Early?"

"You're the one who started this. And I fail to see why we can't *ever* eat *one* meal in peace. You're the most argumentative female I've ever met.''

"Sorry," she mumbled.

"And don't think I believe *that* for a minute, either. You're only saying you're sorry because you're afraid I'll walk out of here and leave you with the bill."

Which he had done on one occasion when she'd pushed him too far. Knowing when to be diplomatic, she asked, "What's the play about, do you know?"

"I don't have any idea. All I know is that there isn't any music in it."

Which was fine with her. He'd taken her to a music hall once and all she could say was that rock music couldn't make its debut any too soon as far as she was concerned. She'd even be willing to welcome Elvis Presley back after what she'd heard that night.

Which was another thing she and Early differed on. She'd tried to get him to listen to her cassettes before her batteries wore out, but he'd likened the music to screaming banshees and wouldn't even tolerate Willie Nelson, whom Lauren thought was ridiculously out of date.

The dinner was the best she'd had in ages—literally ages—but Early closed his hand over hers when she reached for her cigarettes. "Not in the St. Francis" was all he said, and she was forced to sit and watch him smoke while she silently fumed.

The theater had an ornate, high-ceilinged lobby, and the crowd was dressed well enough to put Lauren and Early to shame. Lauren was getting excited about seeing a play. Maybe, if Early was willing, they could make a habit of theatergoing. She'd always preferred movies to plays, but she definitely preferred plays to nothing at all.

She was sure *A Stranger in a Strange Land* sounded familiar, and before the play started she remembered there had been a science fiction book with a title like that. She had read it in college but couldn't recall what it was about.

When the curtain rose and the play began, however, she found out how wrong she'd been. The strangers in the strange land were American Indians. The plot lacked the action of a Western movie, and despite having high hopes, she was quickly bored. The acting was artificial and stilted and the author was preachy.

At the end of the first act she went out to the lobby with Early to have a cigarette—which meant he had a cigarette, not her—and when he asked her if she was enjoying the play, she didn't want to dim his pleasure and said something ambiguous.

"I think it's horrendous" was his opinion.

"Yeah, well I thought so, too, but I didn't want to hurt your feelings."

He cocked an eyebrow at her. "Since when did you become so sensitive to my feelings?"

"I just thought it would be fun to go to the theater once in a while, and I assume the productions aren't all this bad."

"*Hedda Gabler* and *Macbeth* are both playing. We could try one of those if you want."

She saw that she was going to get a classical education in spite of herself. "I'd like to see *Hedda Gabler*," she told him.

"Good. We can try that next week. Although *Macbeth*—"

"I've *seen Macbeth*. My high school put it on one year."

"Oh, well then I can assume you've seen the *definitive* version." With Lauren as his model, Early had honed his sarcasm to perfection.

They usually walked wherever they went, but after the play he took her home in a carriage, the 1906 version of taxis, and she had to admit there was something romantic about being helped into a carriage and having a wrap settled around her. Of course the horse smelled. And the driver. But you couldn't have everything.

She found she was still a little suspicious. A play? Champagne with dinner? Being taken home in a carriage? She was sure that Early was up to something, and if it wasn't marriage, that left only one thing. In a way she wouldn't be averse to a sexual liaison with him; as time went on she found him more and more appealing. But there was a practical consideration: her birth control pills had run out, and she wasn't about to risk pregnancy. Aside from the fact that she wasn't ready for motherhood, there was something about having a baby that would be born in a year predating her own birth that was off-putting to say the least.

But when it came right down to it, she would bet on Early not having the guts to make a move on her. It wasn't that she didn't think he wanted to at times, but in 1906 men were gentlemen, and she had a feeling such things weren't done. At least not with women who hadn't been married, and she was pretty sure Early assumed she was a virgin.

She hoped he wasn't leading up to anything, because if he was, and if she had to turn him down or fight him off or whatever, it would lead to a very frustrating life around the house. Things were good between them now and she didn't want that to change.

Early remained the perfect gentleman on the ride home, but once in the house he asked if she wanted to join him for some brandy. Seated across from him in the living room, she thought she detected a new look in his eyes. It seemed to have something to do with her dress, which he kept eyeing in what he no doubt thought was a surreptitious manner.

Obviously her own clothes didn't turn him on, and when she'd dressed in his mother's he'd probably really been turned off. But now that she was a reasonable facsimile of a woman of the times, he was responding in a manner she found unnerving.

"That was enjoyable tonight," he said, far more polite than he usually spoke to her when they were alone.

"Yes, it was."

"We'll have to do it again."

"Yes, we will." This polite chatter was getting to her. Would the *real* Early please speak up?

"It might not be a bad idea for you to have more of a party dress made up."

"I refuse to waste my money on more clothes, Early."

"Just one. Just to wear when we go out."

"You're talking about a whole month's salary for me, and I prefer to put it to better use."

"Such as?"

"Such as college."

"I don't see how you could possibly get into a college when you have no school records. Or at least that's what you claim, am I right?"

"I thought you could help me."

His eyebrow assumed its upright position. "Oh? Did you think perhaps I'd forge them for you?"

"Something like that."

"I see no reason for you to further your education, Lauren. You have a job now, one that lots of women would love to have. I thought you enjoyed it."

"I do enjoy it, but it doesn't require much mental stimulation. I'm not stupid, Early. I had a good job before and—"

"Don't start on computers again, Lauren."

"I wasn't going to."

"Just what kind of education did you have in mind?"

She didn't have *any* in mind as yet, but she'd think of something just to silence him.

"I thought perhaps science of some kind."

"*Science?*"

"Why do you question everything I say? Why not science? There's going to be all kinds of scientific things in the future that you've never dreamed of, and I thought maybe I could speed things along."

"I just don't know, Lauren..."

"Furthermore, there's going to be a war in a few years, and when that happens there'll be a lot of jobs for women because the men are all going to be over in Europe fighting."

That was the best possible thing she could have said, because once again they were off and running in one of their favorite debates. Early refused to believe that the whole world could go to war at one time, and Lauren, extremely hazy on the facts of World War I, found herself improvising to stimulate the discussion.

Which was all to the good, because an Early engaged in an argument was an Early in an adversary position, and that's just where she wanted to keep him.

Chapter Six

SPOKANE, Wash., Feb. 3—A distinct trembling of the earth occurred here at 5:45 this morning. The shock was felt in many parts of the city. No damage is reported. This is the first earthquake known of definite record here.

THE DAY HAD STARTED OUT so beautifully. When she got up that morning and stuck her head out the window to gauge the temperature, she discovered it was a glorious day. The air felt balmy and even the wind had stilled. It was so warm she might have considered sitting out in the yard in her bikini and trying to get some color, except she knew people were arrested for less than that.

She was in the kitchen fixing herself breakfast when the first shock occurred. She knew exactly what it was when the floor tilted almost imperceptibly and she saw the swaying shadow of the light fixture on the wall. It was only a small tremor, the kind she had experienced countless times, and in those days she would barely have noticed it. She certainly wouldn't have panicked.

But now she found herself running for the door that led to the back yard, huddling within its frame. The tremor was over in seconds, yet she stayed in the doorway until the water on the stove boiled over. She was thinking of the still air that, in Southern California, always presaged an earthquake. She wondered if now she would fear each drop in the wind, and felt a shudder pass through her.

She guessed this was a normal reaction for someone who'd lived through a strong quake, but she was dismayed to see how affected she was by such a minor occurrence. Feeling a little foolish that when it was all over she was still trembling, she sat down at the table and consumed three cups of coffee and smoked six cigarettes before she finally managed to calm herself.

She knew this was something that was going to happen again and again, and she'd have to either get used to it or move away from California. She had an impulse to run down to the *Chronicle* office and tell Early about it, but she didn't want him to think she was the kind of silly female who ran to a male in moments of panic. Because she wasn't that kind of female. She never had been.

By the time she got dressed and was ready to go shopping, the residue of fear that had lingered was gone and she could almost laugh at her reaction. The purpose of her shopping trip helped take her mind off the experience: the item she needed had caused Early his worst siege of embarrassment yet.

It had happened the first time she got her period. Not only did she realize she didn't have anything to use, she hadn't the faintest idea what was around to use in 1906. That was something one never read about in history books. If she'd had a woman to ask, she certainly would have, but the only person she could go to for help was Early. She knew the position she was putting him in, knew that he'd die of embarrassment, but it couldn't be helped. If she didn't find out quickly, she'd soon be in for a worse embarrassment.

It was a Saturday morning and they were having breakfast together before he went in to the office. She had just poured them both their coffee, then casually said, "Early, I have a problem."

He sounded amused when he asked, "What is it this time, Lauren?"

"I started my period." She dug a fork into her omelet and waited for his reaction.

"What's that?"

"My period. I don't know what you call it, but it's what women get every month. You know."

He seemed indeed to know and was turning a darker shade of red than ever before. "If you're having women's problems, Lauren, then I suggest—"

"Early, I just need to know what women use for it these days. Where I come from there are products on the market, but I've never seen anything remotely similar since I've been...since I was...well, since the time change."

Slowly he pushed his plate away, then turned so that his face was hidden from her and said in an extremely strained voice, "You use rags." She could hear him swallow.

"Rags?"

"Yes, rags. And don't ask me how you use them, because I don't want to discuss it." With that he had got up from the table and walked out of the kitchen.

"Early, come back," she shouted after him, but moments later she heard the front door slam. She belatedly realized she should have picked a better moment. One thing Early didn't have was a cast iron stomach.

Lauren found the idea of rags disgusting, but she did use them the first day. Then, that night when she was in bed, she remembered reading somewhere about women in a commune who were using natural sponges. She knew those were around because she had seen them, and on Monday she asked Early if he'd buy some for her. When he asked what she needed sponges for, she told him for cleaning purposes and left it at that. She didn't think there was any reason to embarrass him further.

She had cut them up and found they worked just fine. She didn't like the idea of using the same sponges indefinitely, however, so this fine morning she was going on a shopping expedition to purchase new ones. This time she'd buy them in quantity.

The streets were more crowded than usual, no doubt due in part to the springlike weather. Lauren was walking along, her eyes on the cracked sidewalk to prevent herself from stumbling. She must have seen them moments before they registered in her mind, but it wasn't until they were out of her sight that she realized what she had seen.

Someone in San Francisco was wearing a pair of Adidas!

She started to run, her eyes on the ground as she looked for the shoes again. She rudely shoved her way through crowds of pedestrians, not even bothering to apologize. She couldn't lose the person; she just couldn't. She'd thought she was the only stranger in this strange world, but now she knew she wasn't alone. Someone else had been thrown back in time by the earthquake!

She could feel the adrenaline surging through her as she ran, checking each pair of feet along the way. For some reason she was sure it had been a man wearing them, and yet she knew very well that as many women had worn running shoes in her day. She must have noticed something else—maybe jeans, maybe the whole person—but try as she might, she couldn't remember.

The sponges forgotten, she spent hours in frustrating pursuit of a person who apparently had vanished. Finally, realizing her quarry was lost to her and finding herself near the Chronicle Building, she stopped to tell Early the news. She felt if she wasn't able to share her excitement with someone soon she'd burst.

He was working at his desk and she didn't even apologize for the interruption. She was sure he'd be as excited about it as she was. "I've got to talk to you, Early— it's extremely important. Can you get away to lunch?"

Early looked annoyed. "Can't it wait until I get home tonight?"

She was practically dancing with nervous energy. "If it could wait, I wouldn't be here."

He told her to sit down while he finished what he was working on, and she fidgeted while he slowly and laboriously wrote out his story. She didn't know if she could convey to him what this meant to her, how better it made her feel to know that she wasn't the only one. And another person would be corroboration. Surely two of them could convince Early and everyone else that they were indeed from another time.

Just to have someone to talk to, someone who would understand the things she said, the words she used, the way she thought, would be wonderful. The idea was so exciting that she barely heard Early when he said they could go to lunch now.

She hurried him to the restaurant and picked a table in a quiet corner where they wouldn't be overheard. She could barely contain herself, but as soon as they were seated Early called for a couple of beers, so she waited until the drinks came.

Finally, unable to control herself any longer, she leaned across the table and burst out, "You're not going to *believe* what happened today!"

"I already know."

She was surprised into silence for a moment, then said, "You couldn't know. You couldn't *possibly* know."

Early was nodding. "I didn't feel it, but we heard about it. I was afraid it might've scared you. I even thought of going home to see if you were all right, but then it seemed like such a small one I didn't think you'd be too upset."

In her excitement she had forgotten all about the tremor. She shook her head. "Not that, Early. I wouldn't have bothered you with that."

"I guess I should've gone home. I figured it probably frightened you."

She shook her head impatiently, the tremor of the morning assuming unimportance compared to what she had to tell him now. "Yes, it did, but that doesn't matter. Listen to me, Early, please. I saw someone in Adidas today." She waited for a reaction but he only seemed confused.

"*Adidas*, Early. Running shoes, similar to mine."

He shrugged. "I don't get it."

She leaned across the table, almost upsetting her beer. "Early, someone else from 1987 is back here. I'm not the only one!"

He seemed to recoil a little from her. "You expect me to believe—"

"Damn it, Early, are you calling me a liar?"

Early backed down. "Calm down, Lauren, and tell me what happened."

She settled back in her chair and lit a cigarette. She reminded herself that what she had seen wouldn't mean the same to Early as it did to her. Not nearly the same. "Nothing happened except I saw these shoes in a crowd, but by the time I realized what I'd seen, the person had disappeared. I looked and looked, but I couldn't find him. Or her. It might've been a female, of course."

In a bored tone, Early remarked, "So now you think you have a soul mate around, is that it?"

Deflated by his reaction, she slumped down in her chair and sighed. "I don't know, Early. I guess so. You just can't know what it would mean, though, to have another person around. Someone who understood."

"I understand."

She gave him a scornful look. "You do not. When it comes right down to it, Early Cruz, you don't really believe anything I tell you, and you know it."

"All right, Lauren, forget about what I believe for a moment. Why don't you advertise in the Personal column?"

She threw her head back in delight. "That's a great idea, Early. Whoever it is is bound to read newspapers."

"Write out an ad for me now and I'll make sure it gets in tomorrow's paper."

She smiled at him in gratitude. "Oh, Early, I'm so excited. Can you imagine what this'll mean? I won't be *alone* anymore."

"I wasn't aware that you were," he said.

"Oh, you know what I mean. You've been great, Early, really wonderful, but this will be someone like me. A real person."

His eyes narrowed. "What exactly do you mean by that, Lauren?"

"You know what I mean."

His face was taking on its closed-up look, the one that said she'd gone too far. "Maybe you'd spell it out for me. Are you saying I'm not a real person?"

"I guess I didn't word that very well—"

"I guess you didn't. Then again, maybe you said exactly what you meant." His eyes appeared so dark she couldn't see the pupils.

"It's not that you're not real, Early." She reached out and put her hand on his arm. "See? I can feel you. I know you're real. But you'll never seem *truly* real to me because deep down I know you don't exist anymore."

There was dead silence for a moment, then he spoke, his voice a controlled whisper. "*I'm* the one who doesn't exist?"

"You're like someone I'm seeing in an old movie. A *very* old movie. Someone who's been dead for years and years..." She broke off at the expression on his face.

"Is that the way you think of me?"

Lauren took a drink of her beer, then spent some time lighting a cigarette. Early was looking unaccountably furious, and she wanted to give him a chance to cool off.

"I'm waiting for an answer to my question, Lauren. Is that how you think of me? As a *dead* person?"

"Well, let's face it, Early, what year did you die?"

"How in hell should *I* know," he almost shouted. "I haven't *died* yet!"

"How old are you, Early?"

"Thirty-six."

"Is that all? I thought you were older."

"Well, that's an improvement. A moment ago you thought I was dead."

Lauren took out her calculator and set it on the table, then did a little figuring. "All right, Early, that means in 1987 you'd be a hundred and seventeen. Sorry, but I'm afraid that makes you dead, at least statistically speaking."

"There's one thing you're not taking into account here, Lauren. This happens to be 1906, which means I'm very much alive, and if you're *really* from 1987, like you say you are, that makes you a nothing. A *zero*. You haven't even *arrived* on this fair earth yet, so just who in hell are *you* to tell *me* I'm dead?"

She leaned across the table, locking eyes with his. "Listen, Early, just listen to me. Consciously I never think of you as anything but alive, I swear I don't. But subconsciously I can't help knowing you're not really real. You don't exist. I may have been thrown back here somehow, but somewhere out there 1987 is still going on, and you and everyone else around here are just ancient history."

Early smiled, but the smile didn't reach his eyes. "You must find it strange to be living with some kind of ghost, Lauren."

She stared down at the table, avoiding his eyes. "I do find it strange."

"I'm finding it kind of hard to believe you'd even sit here and *eat* with me."

"As far as that goes, I don't see you ordering any food," she said, matching his sarcastic tone.

"And as far as *that* goes, I think I might prefer to *drink* my lunch today."

"Oh, Early, just when you were doing so well."

"And what in hell is *that* supposed to mean?"

He seemed nearly out of control, and she thought she'd better cool it. "I'm sorry, I didn't mean anything by that, Early."

"Damn it, Lauren, if you don't tell me..."

"It's just that you haven't been drinking so much lately, that's all."

"You telling me how much I can *drink* now?"

Suddenly she'd had it with him. "Go on—get drunk. Be an alcoholic, if that's what makes you happy. *Kill* yourself with booze for all I care."

"What's the difference? I'm dead anyway, according to you."

Lauren got up from the table.

"Where do you think you're going?"

"I'll just go place the ad myself while you sit here and drink yourself into oblivion. Get some of your drinking buddies to keep you company, because *I'm* sure as hell not going to."

"Sit down there—" he started to say, but she ignored him and walked out of the restaurant. Let him sit and get drunk. He was dead anyway. They were all dead. And he'd also managed to kill all the happiness she had been feeling only minutes before.

She stopped in at the Chronicle Building and placed her ad. She knew the wording sounded strange to the clerk who took it from her, and he seemed twice as confused when she told him to run it for a full week, but she wasn't about to explain what it was all about. What did it matter, he was dead, too. For some reason she was being forced to live among a lot of people who thought they existed, but she knew they didn't.

She walked over to Union Square and took a seat on one of the benches. She looked across to where Macy's used to be, then closed her eyes and imagined it there. She pictured spring clothes in the window: dresses with short skirts in rainbow colors; probably resort wear, bathing suits; high-heeled shoes and fragile sandals; costume jewelry in plastic and wood.

She could imagine herself going up the escalator— which, she realized, she hadn't told Early about—and getting off in the junior sportswear department. There would be music playing and the racks would be filled with more clothes than she could wear in a lifetime. She would try some on, and then, if she found something she liked, all she'd have to do would be to take over her charge card and hand it to the salesclerk. Then she'd take her purchase outside to where her car was parked and drive home to her apartment. The phone would probably be ringing and she'd make plans to go out that night. Maybe to a movie, maybe to a club to hear a new group, maybe just to get together with friends and drink a little wine and listen to some music and talk.

She shook her head, then opened her eyes. She hadn't even realized she was crying, but tears were there and she rubbed her eyes dry with her sleeve. She glanced around to see if anyone had noticed, but no one was paying any attention to her.

She was glad she'd seen the person in the running shoes even if she never found him. The sight of the Adidas had managed to jolt her back to reality. She had begun to believe in 1906, to feel a part of it, and she knew that was dangerous. She had even begun to have stronger feelings for Early, and that was the most dangerous of all.

Everything she had said to him was true. He *was* dead. For all intents and purposes he was a ghost. She could no more consider having something going with Early than she could with her great-grandfather. Besides—and this wasn't something she had considered before—her position in 1906 might not be permanent. For all she knew, something might throw her forward into 1987 at any time. She shouldn't have given in, shouldn't have started to settle down. She'd given up any hope of going back to her own time when maybe that hadn't been necessary.

Was there a God? And, if so, was he playing a joke on her? Or on the world of 1906? Did he decide to send her back and see what trouble she could stir up? She gave a little laugh at the way her thoughts were running. If she kept up that line of reasoning, she'd start to think she was a prophet sent back to change history.

She stood up and headed toward home. Poor Early. He never should have got mixed up with her. She knew it was probably as difficult for him as it was for her to live in the same house and not take each other seriously. The house they lived in *looked* real. The bed she slept in *felt* real. And talking to Early in the evenings they spent together usually seemed more meaningful to her than conversations she'd had with any of the men she'd known before. She would've gone crazy if she hadn't given it all some reality.

And yet everything she'd said to him was true. And maybe it was just as well the subject was out in the open, because she had a feeling Early was thinking of her in terms of the future, just as she, in idle moments, had been thinking of him. And a future with Early simply wasn't possible. With a little mental calculation she figured out he was eighty-three years older than she was. She didn't mind a man being a few years older, but eighty-three?

She had a grandfather who was eighty-one. She paused for a moment on the sidewalk and took out her pocket calculator. To her amazement, it turned out that Grandpa would have been born this very year. In 1906. Maybe at this very moment, somewhere in Connecticut, her grandfather was being born. It was actually a possibility that she could travel across the country and find him, then hold him as a baby in her arms.

There was something about the idea that unnerved her, and she quickly thought about something else. She thought about how surprised she'd been when Early told her he was only thirty-six. He looked and acted much older than any thirty-six-year-old she'd ever known, but it must be the times. People must have aged faster in the old days.

She was almost home when she remembered the sponges. Granted, more important things had come up in the interim, but she still needed them, so she turned back and headed for the store.

FOR THE FIRST TIME since she'd lived with him, Early didn't come home that night. When nine o'clock came and went and still no Early, she fixed herself an omelet and ate it at her desk. She worked for a while on her column but finally gave up. She couldn't concentrate. All she could think about was whether the person in the running shoes would see her ad and respond.

Later, when she couldn't get to sleep, she went downstairs and poured herself some brandy. When Early still wasn't home by two, she finally went back to bed. The hell with him. If he wanted to get drunk and sulk like a baby, let him. She had more important things on her mind at the moment than Early's fragile male ego.

Chapter Seven

> Anyone interested in attending a reunion of Sgt. Pepper's Lonely Hearts Club Band, please contact L.H. at the *Chronicle*.

WHEN EARLY ARRIVED home before his usual time the next day, Lauren was ready to apologize. She had purposely stayed away from the *Chronicle* in an effort to avoid him, but as the day wore on she came to the realization that the things she'd said to him had been uncalled for and he had every reason to be angry with her. She had as much as called him a nonentity. If he'd been the one to say something like that to her, if he'd told her that he didn't take her seriously because she didn't actually exist, she knew she would have been twice as upset as Early had been.

Any truce she might have put into effect was postponed, though, because when Early arrived home he wasn't alone. With him was a Chinese woman, and Lauren's first thought was that he had hired an additional maid. Or else he was going to give her her walking papers and she had already been replaced.

"She insisted on seeing you right away," Early began, but then Lauren saw the woman's eyes lighting up, and the next thing she knew she was being hugged ecstatically by the stranger.

Early cleared his throat. "She came in response to your ad," he was saying, but by that time Lauren had caught sight of the tank watch on the woman's wrist and knew why she was there.

"You don't know how happy I am to see you," exclaimed Lauren, beside herself with excitement. She'd found a compatriot—one of her own kind. Realizing they were standing around the entry hall, she said, "Early, why don't you get us all a beer?" then led the woman into the living room, neither of them able to take her eyes off the other for the moment.

"It was you in the Adidas?" asked Lauren, seating herself beside the young woman on the loveseat.

"Adidas? No, I don't have running shoes. I wish I did."

Lauren's eyes widened as she comprehended what that meant. "Then we're not the only ones," she said, going on to explain about seeing the Adidas in the street.

Tears were clouding the woman's dark eyes. "I couldn't believe it when I saw your ad—it was like a miracle. For some reason I thought I was the only one."

"So did I," said Lauren, equally tearful. "It just seemed so weird. I didn't think the same thing could've happened twice."

They contemplated each other in silence for a moment, then Lauren held out her hand and introduced herself. "I'm Lauren Hall," she said and the woman responded, "I'm Cindi Sheung." They were still sitting there shaking hands and grinning at each other when Early appeared with the beer.

He set two glasses and bottles down in front of them, then took a seat across the room. Lauren shot a glance at him and thought he looked like an avid theatergoer who was waiting for the curtain to rise on a new play. Poor Early, the aliens now outnumbered him in his own home.

Cindi took a long drink, then said, "It *was* the earthquake, wasn't it?"

"That was my impression," remarked Lauren. "How bad was it, do you know? I was outside of town at a McDonald's when it happened, and by the time I got to the city it was 1906. Actually, I guess it was right away—the change, I mean. Only I wasn't aware, you know?"

"I know." Cindi's eyes clouded at the memory. "I think it was very bad. At first I didn't even know it was an earthquake. I thought someone had dropped a bomb. I don't know, I guess I was used to thinking more in terms of bombs than earthquakes—I'd been involved in those antinuke demonstrations. Some friends from Oregon were visiting and we were down at Fisherman's Wharf when it happened. Part of a building came down on top of us, and I managed to crawl out, but then I got hit on the head by something else and when I came to..."

Lauren was nodding, remembering her own experience. "How long did it take you to believe it?"

"I *still* don't believe it. I keep thinking I'm going to wake up at any moment." She glanced over at Early. "You know what I mean?"

"Early's not one of us," Lauren told her. Then, seeing Early's expression, she went on, "He's been great—I don't know what I would've done without him. But what

I mean is, he was already here. So how've you been managing?''

"I had the good sense to go to Chinatown, which is the only place I've seen where a woman in pants doesn't look completely out of place. I don't speak Chinese, and very few of them speak much English, but this one family has been very kind to me. I've been working in their laundry for my room and board. Sixteen hours a day, but—'' she spread her hands ''—what're you going to do? I considered myself lucky.''

"Do you read the *Chronicle*?'' Lauren asked.

"All the time.''

"Have you seen that 'Dear Lauren' column?''

Cindi squealed. ''That's *you*? I should've known. The first time I saw it I thought, hey, this is a rip-off of 'Dear Abby,' then I remembered Abby hadn't even been *born* yet. What a great idea that was.''

"Well, I doubt whether I would've been able to do it if Early didn't work for the *Chronicle*. He got me in to see the managing editor—''

"What about dinner?'' Early interrupted.

Lauren looked at Cindi. ''You'll stay, won't you? It'll only be an omelet . . .''

"I'd *die* for an omelet,'' sighed Cindi.

Lauren excused herself, then motioned for Early to follow her into the kitchen. ''Early,'' she said, as soon as they were out of earshot, ''can she stay here?''

"You mean *live* here?'' He sounded startled.

"Please? Just for now?''

"Lauren, she's *Chinese*.''

She put her fists on her hips and glared up at him. "You have some prejudice against the Chinese, Early? You think you're better than they are? With a name like Cruz, I'd think you'd have a little more understanding."

"What's my name got to do with it?"

"The Mexicans haven't had it all that easy, you know."

"*What* Mexicans?" He sounded thoroughly confused now.

"Never mind. I just want to know what you have against the Chinese."

He appeared uncomfortable. "I'm sure they're very hardworking people, Lauren, but . . ."

"But you don't associate with them."

He looked as if he'd rather be anywhere but in the kitchen. "It's just not done, Lauren."

"I don't be*lieve* this! Early, she's American. She doesn't even *speak* Chinese, you heard her. Please. She can live up on the third floor with me and help me with the housework. It'll only be until we can come up with something else. And if she's an embarrassment to you, just tell your nosy neighbors she's the new maid. Or laundress. Tell her she's your Chinese laundress." Now that she and Cindi had found each other, she wasn't about to become parted from her. She was willing to do or say anything to get Early to agree.

"It's nothing personal, Lauren—she seems very nice."

"Oh, thank you, Early," she said before he could say no. Then she gave him a hug that caused him to turn slightly red, and she knew she had gone too far. Stepping back from him, she suggested, "Go in and talk to her while I fix us something to eat, okay? I know you're going to like her when you get to know her.''

He was wearing his downtrodden look as he went to leave, so she added, ''I'm sorry about yesterday, Early.''

He turned back to her. ''No you aren't. You're just saying that to be condescending, because you think you just pulled the wool over my eyes.''

''Honest I'm not. I've been thinking about it all day and the things I said to you were uncalled for. You're a sweetie and I don't know why you put up with me.''

His brows shot up. ''A *sweetie*?''

''Yes, a sweetie. You're just about the nicest man I've ever known.''

He was starting to smile. ''Don't be so sure I'm a 'sweetie,' Lauren. It just might be that I have ulterior motives.''

But before she could ask him *what* ulterior motives, he was out of the kitchen, and she decided not to pursue the subject. Anyway, she was too excited about Cindi's arrival to worry about Early—*or* his ulterior motives. And she was pretty sure ulterior motives in 1906 weren't the same as ulterior motives in 1987. Early was a gentleman through and through.

In all the years since college, Lauren had never felt any desire for a female roommate, but now that she'd found Cindi she wasn't about to let her go. She was reminded of a vacation she had taken in Mexico one year. The first few days she had been happy to be alone, to relax on the beach during the day and retire to her hotel room at night after a late dinner. But then, about her fifth day there, she was beginning to talk to herself, and when another

American woman showed up at the hotel, Lauren greeted her like a long lost friend. They didn't have anything in common, and if Lauren had met her in San Francisco they wouldn't have become friends, but for the rest of the trip she was so thankful to have someone to speak English with that she forgave the woman all her faults.

It was the same with Cindi, except that she felt she and Cindi would have been friends if they'd met in 1987. Lauren was in such a hurry to talk to her again, to compare notes on their experiences, that she didn't take much time with the omelets and didn't even bother to set the table. She just carried the plates into the living room on a tray and ignored Early's quizzical look when he saw they were going to eat there.

"We *do* have a dining room," he pointed out.

"Oh, Early, in 1987 *everyone* ate in the living room—usually while watching television."

"Speak for yourself," said Cindi.

"*You* know about television, too?" he asked Cindi.

Cindi glanced from Early to Lauren and then back to Early. "You don't believe her, do you?"

He shrugged, a doubtful look on his face.

"Wait," Cindi told him, "we'll convince you."

"I admit it's hard not to believe all the proof," Early began, "but..."

"You have *proof*?" Cindi asked Lauren.

Lauren was nodding. "Unfortunately, most of it requires batteries—like the Sony Walkman—but I had my driver's license and money and some other stuff."

"How fantastic! I lost my purse during the earthquake, I guess, and didn't have anything but what I was wearing."

"Are those the clothes?" Lauren asked, nodding her head toward Cindi's pants and jacket.

"Would you believe this is what the Chinese wear today?"

"I wouldn't mind dressing like that," said Lauren. "I've been wearing these uncomfortable long dresses."

"And you'll continue to wear them unless you decide to move to Chinatown," announced Early.

Lauren decided if that was a hint for her to leave with Cindi, she'd ignore it.

When Early excused himself to go to his Thursday-night card game, Lauren barely noticed him leave. But as soon as she heard the front door close, she said to Cindi, "It's okay with Early for you to stay here."

"You really mean it?"

Lauren nodded. "It's a huge house and I've fixed up the third floor for myself. All we have to do is drag another mattress up."

"You don't know what heaven that'll be. I've been sharing this one-room house with three adults and six children. But I don't want to just disappear on those people. They've been very good to me and I want to thank them. I'd also like to pick up my regular clothes."

Lauren hadn't seen 1906 Chinatown yet, so she went along with Cindi when she collected her things. As they walked through the narrow, dimly lit streets, she was appalled at the poverty she saw all around her. More shocking was the house, no more than a shack, really, where Cindi had been living since the earthquake. She didn't say anything until they had left the house; she was about to mention the squalor when something held her back. Maybe the people in Chinatown in 1987 lived like that and she hadn't been aware of it. But she was sure that couldn't be possible.

It was Cindi who brought up the subject. "I wish I could do something for those people. If nothing else, at least assure them that someday things will be better for them."

"Did they understand why you were leaving?"

"I think they thought I was going to work for you. They seemed happy for me, so I guess being a servant is considered better than working in a laundry."

They couldn't seem to stop talking, even for a moment. All the way back to Early's house they told each other about their respective lives before the quake, finding they had both gone to the same places in the city and marveling that they hadn't met each other. Cindi was twenty-five and had worked as an adjuster in an insurance office while she studied commercial art at night. She had lived in the Marina district but had frequented some of the same clubs as Lauren. They went so far as to list the various men they had dated and came up with one in common.

"But I guess any two women in San Francisco could do that," said Cindi, alluding to the large gay population.

They both agreed Ed had been a loser, but Lauren could only nod when Cindi remarked she'd even take *Ed* now.

Back at the house, Lauren grabbed a bottle of wine and they went up to the third floor, where Lauren showed off her living quarters.

"Pick any room," Lauren offered, "and it's yours."

"If you don't mind, I'd just as soon share yours tonight," said Cindi.

"Great—we'll have an old-fashioned slumber party."

They had brought up another mattress and were dressed in Lauren's nightgowns, still drinking and reminiscing, when Lauren heard Early come home. She checked her watch and saw that it was after two, but she didn't care. She and Cindi would stay up talking all night if they felt like it; nothing prevented them from sleeping the next day if they wanted.

She was quite drunk and becoming maudlin when she asked Cindi, "Why do you think it happened?"

"You mean us sent back in time?"

Lauren nodded.

"It's creepy, isn't it? You want to hear my theory?"

"I'm impressed you even have one. Nothing I've thought of makes any sense at all—unless that particular McDonald's was built in the middle of some Bermuda Triangle thing, and I really don't believe in that stuff. Although I'll tell you, Cindi—now I wish I'd read more science fiction. Maybe I'd know how to build a time machine and get back."

"Well, the only thing that makes any sense to me, Lauren, is the year, but I suppose you've thought of that."

Lauren propped herself on one elbow. "The year? What're you talking about?"

"1906."

"That makes sense to you? I don't get it."

"You mean you don't *know*?"

"Know what?"

Cindi leaned across the space between the mattresses and put a hand on Lauren's shoulder. "It's the year of the big earthquake, honey. The one that demolished the city."

Lauren's mouth fell open. "The *San Francisco* earthquake?"

"The very one."

Lauren sat up. "My God, Cindi—we've got to get out of here."

"I don't think there's any rush."

"What do you mean? No *way* am I going to live through another one of those." She started to get up off the mattress, but Cindi pulled her back.

"Hey, it's not going to happen tomorrow. As I recall, it was in the summer sometime. Anyway, I've got this theory—"

"Are you sure about this?" Lauren interrupted in a sudden panic. "Are you sure it was 1906?"

Cindi nodded. "I grew up here, Lauren. They really drilled that date into us in school."

Lauren could feel her heart pounding. "Just when I thought I was learning to cope, now this. *Why*? Why should we have to go through *two* of them? I've got to tell Early. He's got to warn everyone in the newspaper, get people to leave the city." She jumped up and looked down at Cindi. "Listen, I've really got to tell him. I'll be right back."

"Can't it wait until morning?"

"No—no, it can't. God, this is terrible. We've got to *do* something."

Heedless of disturbing Early in the middle of the night, and equally heedless of the picture she presented in her nightgown, Lauren grabbed one of the oil lamps and padded barefoot downstairs. The door to Early's room was shut, and she opened it and walked inside.

Except for the first night she was there and Early, in passing, had pointed it out to her, she had never really seen his room. One glance told her how neat he was in comparison to her. Snoring loudly and smelling of booze, he was lying on his back in the large bed, his arms flung out at his sides. "Early," she said, poking him in the chest, "wake up!"

"What? What's the matter?" he mumbled, but his eyes weren't open and she thought he was still sleeping.

"Early, you've got to wake up!" She set the lamp down on the bedside table and shook him by both shoulders. *"Early, please."*

His eyes opened, squinting in the light. He closed them, then opened them again. "Lauren?"

"Please, Early, could you sit up a minute?"

He shoved the pillow against the headboard and slid himself up a few inches, his eyes on her body beneath the gown. Realizing for the first time how she was dressed, she crossed her arms over her chest and stared down at him. "You awake now, Early?"

His usually neat hair was rumpled, and the sheet slid down to reveal his bare chest. Then she saw the look in his eyes, a look that gave her goose bumps, and she backed away from the bed.

"Come here and let me touch you, Lauren, so I know I'm not dreaming." His voice was low, almost a whisper.

"Please, Early—"

"God, just look at you. Put your arms back down so I can see you again. I've dreamed of this...so many times."

Lauren was having trouble believing it was Early saying those things. "Early, don't start something now. I don't get it. We've been alone in this house for *weeks* and you've never talked like this."

"You never came to my bedroom before."

"I came because I had something to tell you. It's important, Early, or I wouldn't have bothered you. I guess I made a mistake."

His attention appeared to be focused more on her transparent nightgown than on her words. "Hand me a cigarette, will you, please?"

She picked up his cigarettes from the nightstand and passed them to him, taking one for herself. As she bent forward to get a light from him, he took hold of her wrist and pulled her down on the bed beside him. "What're you doing, Early—let *go* of me!"

"What I'd like to know is what *you're* doing coming into my bedroom in the middle of the night dressed like a tart." His voice conveyed danger.

She broke out of his grasp and grabbed the bedspread off his bed, wrapping it around her. "If I were looking for *sex*, Early, I would've been a little more subtle."

His eyes were mocking. "When were you ever subtle, Lauren?"

"Damn it, Early, I'm not the least interested in sex with you. You're older than my grandfather." Which wasn't exactly the truth. The idea of sex with Early had crossed her mind on occasion, usually when she was alone in bed at night.

His eyes narrowed. "I don't know how old your grandfather is, but I'm feeling pretty young at the moment. You want me to prove it?"

She hugged the bedspread tighter and stared at him in dismay. "Early, you've got it all wrong. Please, just listen to me, okay?"

He was starting to smile. "Come over here where we can talk."

"Forget it, you're drunk. I'll tell you in the morning."

"I'm pretty sober at the moment."

"Well, I'm not. We'll talk in the morning, okay, Early?"

"We'll talk now." His voice was a command.

With a sigh of exasperation, Lauren grabbed one of the chairs and dragged it closer to his bed, but not close enough so that he could touch her again. "This is really important, Early, or I wouldn't have disturbed your sleep. Just this moment Cindi reminded me about the earthquake—"

"The hell with the earthquake! I know more about that earthquake of yours than I want to know."

"Not that one. I wouldn't have bothered you about that. It's the 1906 earthquake I'm talking about. The *big* one. The one that destroyed San Francisco."

He held up one hand. "Whoa! Slow down a minute. Are you telling me that Cindi said there's going to be a big earthquake this year?"

"There *is* going to be."

"Am I to assume we now have a Chinese soothsayer living with us?" He was almost laughing. "An Eastern mystic?" He was making her furious.

"Forget it," she said, standing up and heading for the door. "I'll explain it to you later, after you've sobered up."

"Lauren!" His voice called after her.

She turned around at the door. "What?"

"Don't ever come into my bedroom again. Not unless you mean it."

His tone was forbidding, and she found herself slamming the door when she left, then running up to the third floor as fast as her feet would carry her.

"What happened?" asked Cindi when Lauren threw herself down on her mattress.

"He thought I went down there to seduce him."

"You mean you two aren't, uh..." Cindi started wriggling her eyebrows.

"No, we aren't."

"He's a sexy guy, Lauren. What's the problem?"

"What's the *problem*? The *problem* is, he's older than my own grandfather. Maybe *you* don't consider that a problem, but *I* sure as hell do."

"It's just as well, because he won't be around long,'' remarked Cindi in a sober voice.

"What do you mean? I plan on convincing him to get out of here before the earthquake."

"You really care for him, huh?"

"It's not only him. I'm going to try to get everyone out. We can't just sit back and let it happen without warning people."

"I still haven't told you my theory," said Cindi. "I've given this a lot of thought, and what I think—I think when the next quake hits we'll be sent back to '87."

Lauren sat up and grabbed hold of Cindi's hand. *"What?"*

"I mean it. It makes as much sense as anything. If one big quake can send us back in time, why can't the next send us forward?"

"I don't believe that," Lauren disagreed.

"Why not?"

"Because I didn't believe it the first time. Twice would be too much. I don't know about you, but I'm going to get out of here. Maybe L.A."

"I'll bet you I'm right."

"It's a nice fantasy, Cindi, but I don't think it's based in reality."

"Nothing *about* this whole thing is based in reality. But I have a feeling, Lauren—a really strong feeling—that I'm right about this. I think I'll go back."

"Are you psychic?"

"Not that I know of. But I'm telling you, I really believe it."

Lauren sighed. "Go back to what? If the earthquake was that big, there might not be a California anymore."

"So I show up in Nevada instead. I'd still rather be in 1987 than here. Wouldn't you?"

"Of course I would, but the idea of having to live through another earthquake scares me to death. I think a second experience like that would drive me round the bend."

Cindi gave her a sly look. "I think you don't want to leave Early."

"Don't be ridiculous, Cindi. He's been a good friend to me, that's all."

"From where I'm sitting it looks like a lot more than friendship."

"He's not my type."

"I can remember a time in San Francisco when if I met a guy who was straight, he was my type."

Lauren laughed. "So can I. And Early's straight, all right, but there's something about getting involved with a man from the past that I can't handle."

"I can relate to that. He could turn out to be your great-great-grandfather or something."

"No, I thought of that, but my relatives were all from the east."

"Well, if you're really not interested, my advice to you is to watch it, because he's for darn sure interested in you."

"No he's not."

"I saw the way he looked at you."

"Cindi, you've only been here one night, I see him all the time. He'd been drinking tonight, and my showing up in his bedroom didn't help a lot, but believe me, the best you could say for us is that we manage to coexist.''

''You know what, Lauren?''

''What?''

''Maybe there're a lot of us. Maybe all over California there are survivors of the quake who got thrown back, just like us.''

Lauren's eyes lit up with excitement. ''We ought to try to find out. Maybe we could put ads in other California papers.''

''It'd be worth a try,'' said Cindi.

''And if we found others, we could form a commune.''

''You can. I intend on going back. Or forward, I guess. But in the meantime, yeah, let's do it. I feel like I've got to do *something* positive or go nuts. But oh, you can't know how thankful I am to have you here. My eyes almost popped out of my head when I saw your ad. At first I thought it might be some kind of coincidence, that maybe there was a band with the same name.''

''I made that up on the spur of the moment,'' Lauren told her. ''I probably could've done better.''

''No. It was fine. Only...''

''Only what?''

''What if some old people got thrown back? People who didn't know the Beatles' music? Or kids? Little kids?''

''We'll have to do more. Maybe we could post bills all over, the way they do when a kid is missing.''

Cindi was getting excited. "Yes, that's it. And I can make them, I know how to do that. Maybe you could even get an article put in the *Chronicle*."

Lauren shook her head. "No, I don't think so. If Early doesn't believe me, and he really doesn't, no one else at the paper will. They think I'm a little eccentric as it is. But we ought to reach plenty of people with posters."

"I'm psyched," said Cindi. "We're going to do it, Lauren. If there are any other survivors out there, we're going to find them. Listen, you have access to a typewriter?"

"There are a few at the *Chronicle* offices. The reporters don't use them, but the clerks do. I'm sure I'd be able to type up stuff there."

"And if we can get hold of something to make signs out of, I can do the artwork."

"I know an art supply store where we can get everything we need. I have money, too."

"Are you tired, Lauren?"

"Not a bit. What about you?"

"Me, neither. Let's start composing the poster now. God, you've made me want to *live* again. For a while there, the first few days, I was thinking I'd rather be dead."

"Oh, no, Cindi."

"Honest. You don't know how bad the Chinese have it in 1906."

"I was thinking that tonight. Maybe we ought to try to do something for them."

"Like civil rights?"

Lauren nodded.

"I thought about that. I'll tell you what, if I'm proved wrong, if the earthquake doesn't send us back, I think we ought to do something. Not only for the Chinese, either—for women, too."

"I've been trying to do that in my column," Lauren told her.

"Yeah, I noticed. That surprised me. I couldn't believe someone that hip was writing a column in 1906."

Lauren stood up. "Come on, let's go down to the kitchen and I'll make some coffee. We've got work to do."

They were still at it when Early left for work that morning. He had peered into the kitchen, seen them, then the next thing they heard was the front door closing.

"I think he's mad at me again," observed Lauren.

"Not mad, just frustrated," teased Cindi.

"Cindi, will you knock it off?"

But Cindi just made an inscrutable face and said, "Just wait and see, Lauren, that's all I can say. You know my feeling about going back to '87 in the next earthquake? Well, my feeling about you and Early getting together is just as strong. Maybe stronger."

"And I say you're wrong about both," announced Lauren, determined to have the last word.

Chapter Eight

If you remember Macy's and McDonald's, you're not alone. Please contact L.H. at the *Chronicle*.

"THAT OUGHT TO DO IT," said Cindi, perusing the ad in the paper. "I defy anyone to have lived around here in the eighties and not known Macy's and McDonald's."

"More coffee?" asked Lauren.

"Please."

"That ad didn't sound as bizarre as the first one, either," observed Lauren. "The clerk who took it didn't even look confused. After all, Macy and McDonald could be people. Well, I guess they *were* people at one time, weren't they?"

"Maybe they still are. Were. Oh, hell, do you have as much trouble with tenses as I do?"

Lauren grinned. "I keep thinking of them as real time and fantasy time, but I could have the two mixed up. You want to hear a *really* weird theory I came up with once? I thought maybe I was crazy and had been here all the time and 1987 was just some hallucination I'd gone through."

"Yes, but I disprove that theory. Two of us wouldn't have had the same hallucination."

"I didn't believe it anyway. I thought it up, but I didn't believe it. Anyway, it would be pretty hard to halluci-nate a Sony Walkman."

"I wish it still worked. I'd die to hear some real music."

"There's probably a way to convert it to electricity," said Lauren, "but I don't have the slightest idea how."

"Maybe there's some electrical whiz from 1987 running around out there. And the sooner we post the bills, the sooner we're going to find out. I have an idea I shouldn't look Chinese when we do it, though."

"Why not?"

"I'm not sure, Lauren, but I have a feeling the Chinese stay in Chinatown. Anyway, we don't want any trouble. For all we know it might be against the law to nail these up."

They went upstairs and sorted through Lauren's clothes. Cindi was slightly smaller than her, but not much, and Lauren's new dress fit her quite well. With her long hair piled on top of her head beneath Early's mother's hat, Cindi more closely resembled a woman from 1906 than Lauren did.

"You can wear my sunglasses," Lauren suggested.

"Sunglasses weren't around—aren't around—at the moment."

"Well, if you don't want to look Chinese..."

When they finally set out, Cindi was wearing the sunglasses and Lauren was wrapped in the concealing cape, even though the weather was too warm for it. A lot of curious stares came their way as they nailed their notices to trees, electricity poles and the sides of wooden buildings, but no one actually stopped them. They were pretty sure some of the notices would be torn down, but by putting up so many, they figured they had a good chance of reaching those who would understand their message.

It hadn't been easy making up more than a hundred notices by hand. Cindi had had the idea for the picture. Filling up most of each posterboard was an illustration of a TV set, complete with rabbit-ear antenna. On each screen was a cleverly drawn Miss Piggy, and underneath, in large letters, the announcement: Meeting of Miss Piggy Fan Club At. In small letters at the very bottom they had printed Early's address. They were in agreement that anyone from 1987 would instantly notice a picture of a TV screen, even if he or she didn't know who Miss Piggy was.

They had wondered about putting their address on the signs but thought it was a better idea than having strange people arrive at the *Chronicle* office. Early didn't have a telephone, but even if he did, they weren't sure survivors would have the money to use a phone to call them. Or even find one. So far Lauren hadn't noticed telephone booths anywhere. They decided that once the notices were posted, one of them would be home at all times in case someone arrived.

They spent all day going around the city tacking the posters up. Sometimes they took the cable cars but more often walked. At one point, when Cindi tripped on her skirt going up a curb, she said, "You know something, Lauren? If I don't get thrown back to '87, I have half a mind to become a fashion designer."

Lauren was nodding in agreement. "That crossed my mind, too."

"I mean it. I bet if we really did it right, we could move fashions up by a good fifty years."

"When did women start wearing pants, do you know?"

Cindi shrugged. "I don't have the slightest idea. But they were wearing them in a lot of the old movies I've seen on television."

"I like that Chinese outfit of yours," Lauren remarked.

"Mmm, it's comfortable."

"If I looked Chinese, I'd go around in that."

"I bet you could pass for Chinese," Cindi told her. "Just dye your hair black, pull it back in a small pigtail and put on some eye liner."

"You think that would fool anyone?"

Cindi chuckled. "It wouldn't fool anyone Chinese, but I bet it'd fool anyone else. Nobody looks very closely at a Chinese person on the streets. You'd have to walk kind of bent over and take smaller steps, that's all. And act properly subservient if anyone speaks to you."

"It'd be worth it if I could wear pants on the street. You know how to sew?"

"Sure, I learned in high school. Didn't you?"

Lauren shook her head. "I flunked home ec. Early's mother had a sewing machine. You think you could use it?"

"I could try. Did they have electric ones now?" She laughed. "See what I mean about tenses?"

"I don't know if it's electric, I haven't taken a look at it. But I doubt it."

"Well, if I can figure it out, we're in business."

Time and Again

THAT WAS SATURDAY, and Lauren hadn't spoken to Early since Thursday night. Or early Friday morning, to be more exact. When she stopped by the *Chronicle* office on Friday he was either out or hiding, she didn't know which, and that night he hadn't come home until late. She and Cindi had been up on the third floor making the posters, and something stopped her from going downstairs and confronting him.

She hadn't had a lot of time to herself since Cindi's arrival, but when she did have a few moments they were devoted to thoughts of Early. She realized belatedly what a dumb thing she had done by going down to his bedroom in a thin nightgown. Any guy in his right mind would have got the wrong impression from that. She sure would have, if Early had suddenly shown up in her bedroom wearing only his jockey shorts or whatever it was men wore now.

She would have jumped to the natural conclusion that it was sex he was after. Why else appear like that? He had no way of knowing she was waking him up to announce an imminent earthquake. That was probably the *last* thing on his mind.

So she couldn't fault him for coming on to her. And he'd been great to her all along. He'd taken her in, helped get her a job, even allowed Cindi to move in. The poor guy had been peacefully living alone all that time, and now, because of her, he was practically running a rooming house for earthquake survivors from 1987.

And when it came right down to it, she would have been pretty miffed if he *hadn't* found her sexy. If she had deliberately gone down there with the intention of entic-

ing him, and he hadn't come on to her, she would've hit
the ceiling.

"The poor, misunderstood guy" was Cindi's assessment. Cindi, of course, thought she should go for it, enjoy her time while in 1906. Of course Cindi didn't believe
they were going to *stay* in 1906.

"Come on," she had said, "none of this is real, so why
not do whatever you want? What's it going to hurt?"

"For starters, I'm out of birth control pills," noted
Lauren.

Cindi shrugged. "So what?"

"So what? How can you say that? Would *you* want to
have a kid who's older than you?"

"Really, Lauren, do you honestly think you can get
impregnated by a man who's no longer alive?"

"He seems pretty real to me."

"Yeah, but think about it. It just wouldn't work out.
Realistically, you can't have a kid who's older than you,
so obviously you can't get pregnant."

"That might make sense to you, Cindi—"

"It's the way it works, Lauren. Haven't you ever read
any science fiction?"

"Not much. I think I read a couple of Heinleins in
college. Why, have you?"

"Yes, and the one recurring theme is that you can't
change history."

"Well, that's pure baloney, Cindi, because I've already changed history."

"How?"

Lauren gave her a triumphant look. "By writing that
column, for one. If we get sent back to 1987, like you

think we will, we'll be able to go to the library and look up the *Chronicle* and find that column written by me. Explain that!''

''I can explain it.''

''Yeah? Let's hear you.''

''It's just possible that the earthquake will destroy all copies of the *Chronicle*.''

''No way, Cindi. It gets sent out of the city, even to L.A. You know something? If we get back, we'll have proof we've been here.''

''No one will believe us.''

''I know. Early doesn't believe me now, even with the evidence right in front of his eyes. Maybe we should think of some way we could really prove it.''

''The best proof, the only kind anyone will believe,'' said Cindi, ''is if we get our pictures in the newspaper. At least *you* could. You could get them to print a picture next to your column.''

''Yeah, but the only thing is, I don't believe we're going to get back.''

''We have to, Lauren. Nothing else makes any sense. Listen, I'm twenty-five now, which means in 1987 I'll be...what will I be?''

''A hundred and six,'' announced Lauren, after using her calculator.

''No, wait a minute, that's not what I mean. I was born in 1962. How old will I be then?''

''Eighty-one,'' Lauren answered.

''See what I mean? I could conceivably live till I'm eighty, but that would mean I'd still be alive when I was being born. Those kinds of things won't work, Lauren. We've *got* to go back."

"Either that or die young."

"And do what, be reincarnated?"

"That doesn't make sense, either."

"No, it doesn't," agreed Cindi.

"Thinking about it drives me nuts."

"Me, too."

"Then let's not think about it" was Lauren's final word.

"But getting back to Early..."

"The hell with Early. I've got enough problems without getting involved with a ghost. At least you're here now, that should help. When it was just me and Early I might've been tempted, but not anymore. The whole thing's too confusing."

WHEN EARLY CAME HOME from work that day, Lauren went downstairs alone. She told Cindi she needed to talk to him, maybe apologize for waking him up on Thursday the way she had. She wanted to set things right so there wouldn't be a strain between them. Anyway, the poor guy was obviously trying to stay away from his own house, and that wasn't fair.

He was hanging his raincoat on the coatrack in the hall when Lauren came down the stairs. She saw him look at her then turn away.

"I think we should talk, Early."

"I agree," was all he said.

"Would you like some coffee? A drink?"

"A little whiskey, I think. Will you join me?"

So he was going to be formal, was he? She followed him into the living room and waited while he poured them each a whiskey, sans ice, of course. There were no such things as ice cubes, and Early had demurred when she had suggested keeping the whiskey in the icebox.

He sat down in one of the chairs and she sat across from him on the love seat. They both lit cigarettes, then Early said, "I think I should—"

"No," she cut him off, "there's no reason for you to apologize."

The corner of his mouth rose. "I had no intention of apologizing, Lauren. I don't feel I have anything to apologize *for*."

Well, so much for thinking he was the *compleat* gentleman. "Well, I want to apologize to you."

"Good." His tone was smug.

"You're not making this any easier, Early."

"I'm listening, Lauren—go on."

"You've been really great, Early—"

"Yes, a 'sweetie,' if I recall correctly."

Lauren flashed him a look of annoyance. "Will you just let me get on with it, Early?"

"Please."

She started again. "I apologize, Early. You had every right to jump to the wrong conclusion when I came into your bedroom the other night."

"Every right."

"Yes, that's what I said. I have to admit you surprised me a little. I mean, I didn't think men in 1906 came on that strong..."

"They do when women enter their bedrooms as scantily clad as you were."

"Yes. Well, I wasn't thinking. The business about the earthquake had me so excited I couldn't wait to tell you. To warn you."

"And I mistook your intentions. I'm not going to apologize for that, Lauren. I won't even plead too much drink, although there was that. What I'm trying to say is, even though you may think of me as a ghost, I'm quite human, you know. I've also grown to care for you despite the fact that ninety-nine percent of the time you're trying to annoy me."

"I like you too, Early. In fact I consider you my best friend."

Early didn't appear thrilled at the news. "Why don't you consider Cindi your best friend instead and reserve something else for me?"

"What are you getting at, Early?"

"What I'm getting at, Lauren, is that I thought, in time, we'd become more to each other than friends."

"How much time?"

The brow went up. "Are you in some kind of hurry?"

Lauren sighed. "Early, you want to hear what Cindi thinks?"

"I doubt it."

"Well, she thinks that the next quake is going to send us back to 1987. Which means we don't have much time."

"And do you concur with that theory?"

She shook her head. "No. I think it's too farfetched."

"I'd like to hear about this earthquake."

"I didn't think you believed me."

"I don't know *what* I believe anymore, Lauren. I found you intriguing with all your talk of 1987, but I never really believed it. I wanted to, but...well, the truth is, I have trouble believing in *any*thing that firmly. But now, with Cindi...well, I don't know how there could be two originals loose in San Francisco."

"You do believe us?"

"Let's just say I'm willing to listen."

"Oh, Early, I'm so glad to hear that because you've got to help us. We've got to warn everyone to get out of the city."

"Just when is this quake supposed to occur?"

"Cindi thinks in the summer, but she's not positive. It could be sooner for all we know. But it was devastating, Early. It destroyed almost the entire city. There was even a movie made about it with Clark Gable that they play on the Late Show sometimes, but I've never seen it."

"Were many people killed?"

"Cindi says not. She thinks it was mostly the buildings that were destroyed. But *some* will be killed unless we do something about it."

"And what do you suggest, that we move the entire population of San Francisco down to Los Angeles?"

"Don't be sarcastic, Early. We have to do *some*thing. And no one will believe us, but they might believe you. I thought maybe you could start writing a series of articles about the dangers of earthquakes and how scientists are predicting a big one for this year."

"You know H.H. better than that. He'd never allow it. And while I might believe you a little, no one else will."

"If we could start small, then...maybe with discussion groups. If we could get some of the people out and the rest of them prepared, well, that should help."

"You, I take it, are one of the ones getting out?"

"I'm not staying around for another earthquake. We can at least get away as far as Carmel, then return after the quake if you want."

"I'm not leaving, Lauren."

"Early! You've got to!"

"What you seem to be forgetting is that I'm a reporter. Do you think I'd leave the city right before a story of that size?"

"You're not going to be able to write it if you're dead!"

"San Francisco has had earthquakes before, Lauren, and it will again. I'm staying."

"Why are you so stubborn?

"If it will make you feel any better, I'll put the house in your name. That way if I'm killed in the quake, you'll have a place to come back to."

"Thanks for nothing. This house will probably go like all the rest."

He smiled. "Well, then, maybe when this big quake comes, I'll be thrown forward in time and we'll meet in 1987."

Lauren sighed. "You really don't believe me, do you?"

"I don't know *what* I believe anymore."

"WHAT HAPPENED when you talked to him?" Cindi asked her later that night.

Cindi had cooked a Chinese dinner, which they all had thoroughly enjoyed, then afterward they had played poker together at the dining room table. Lauren and Cindi had regaled Early with stories about single life in the eighties, Cindi going so far as to explain to Early about San Francisco being the gay capital of the world.

"I've always thought it was quite gay now," remarked Early in all innocence.

Cindi glanced at Lauren. "Should I tell him?"

"Go ahead. I didn't have the heart to."

When Early finally understood the new meaning of "gay," he said, "I guess that means if the earthquake shoots me forward into 1987, I'll have to like boys, is that it?" And for the first time Cindi was treated to the sense of humor that resided just below the surface of his usually serious demeanor.

When they were in bed later, and Cindi asked about their talk, Lauren told her that Early wouldn't help them. "I don't think he really believes there's going to be a bad quake. And even if there is, he's staying."

"I am, too. You're the one who's going away to avoid it."

"What are you going to do, Cindi, go down to Fisherman's Wharf and hope you get thrown forward in time?"

"What's so crazy about that?"

"What's crazy, Cindi, is that you might end up in the ocean. We don't know how extensive that quake was."

"Look, Lauren, I like you, and I'll miss you if I go back and you don't. But right now I have family I miss, and friends. And I want to be a commercial artist. I also miss hot water and microwave ovens and a whole lot of other things. Don't you?''

"Sure I do, but if you want to know the truth, I like doing this column better than I liked my job before. I even have ideas for other columns I could do."

"And you also like Early."

"Listen, Cindi, if I had a real choice I'd go back. But I don't have a choice, so I'm going to try to make the best of it, that's all."

THE NEXT DAY Early asked Lauren if she'd like to accompany him to his cousins' house for Sunday dinner. Lauren, who didn't even know Early had a cousin, said no right away, without even thinking that maybe she wasn't being polite.

"I see," Early said.

"Nothing personal," she assured him, "it's just that we want to be here in case someone notices our posters and comes over."

"You don't need to wait around," Cindi told her. "I'll be here. Go on with Early if you want."

Lauren shot Cindi a glance that said to stay out of it, but Cindi wasn't even looking at her. "What'll you do all day by yourself?"

"Are you kidding? For starters, I'll wash my hair. Then I think I'll take a look at the sewing machine you mentioned. If I can work it, I'll start taking in some of those clothes. Listen, don't worry about me. Up until now I've been working seven days a week. Doing nothing would be a luxury."

After that, Lauren couldn't very well say she didn't want to eat dinner with Early's cousins, although she didn't. She went upstairs and put on her dress, then let Cindi help fasten her hair up beneath a hat so she wouldn't appear too strange to the cousins.

When they were out on the sidewalk, Early took her hand and placed it on his arm. She gave him a look of surprise. She'd seen all the other couples walking that way, but up until now Early hadn't done so. Which meant, if she was not mistaken, that he was now embarking on a courtship—and she was the courted.

"I thought I was supposed to be your niece," she said, noting Early's nods to neighbors as they passed.

"I don't think anyone believed that."

"Why not? Why couldn't I be your niece?"

"They've seen us going out together too often to maintain that fiction. And if you *were* my niece, and you were looking for a husband, I would have introduced you to young men by now."

"Don't let the fact that I'm not your niece stop you, Early," she joked.

But he countered, "That's not what's stopping me, Lauren."

She was about to reply, then decided not to pursue the subject. From what she knew of the era, courting could take a good long time. In fact a very long time. She ought to be out of San Francisco and in Los Angeles before he even shifted into high gear.

When Early turned into a walk leading to a fancy house on Nob Hill, Lauren commented, "You didn't tell me they were rich."

"You didn't ask. But they're not rich, just well off."

"In my day you'd have to be rich to live here."

Early stopped in midstride. "One thing, Lauren. When we get inside, please don't refer to *your* day. Am I making myself clear?"

"Perfectly."

A properly attired maid let them in, then Lauren was introduced to Cousin Charles and his wife, Elizabeth. Once they were seated in the parlor—and this was a room even Lauren wouldn't consider a living room—their two teenage daughters were brought in and presented, and Lauren found herself hoping they'd stay. They looked like a lot more fun than Charles and Elizabeth.

While Charles and Early discussed world events, or—from Lauren's point of view—ancient history, Elizabeth politely questioned Lauren on her own ancient history, and no matter how many beseeching glances Lauren threw Early's way, he wouldn't come to her rescue.

Finally, finding the entire experience outrageous anyway, Lauren manufactured a childhood in France. As she was speaking she suddenly remembered the old skits on *Saturday Night Live* about the family of Coneheads from outer space, who, when asked, always swore they came from France. She started to smile and was afraid she was going to burst out laughing.

"What are they wearing in Paris these days," asked one of the daughters, and Lauren instantly answered, "Pants."

At Elizabeth's shocked expression, she amended "At least around the house. The latest thing for entertaining at home are wide-legged pants and blousy tops."

Elizabeth didn't seem enchanted with the notion, but
then Elizabeth had extremely wide hips. The girls,
though, insisted that Lauren draw them a sketch, which
she did, thinking all the while that maybe Cindi could
make up some outfits like that and they could advertise
them in the *Chronicle* as the latest from Paris. If she
made enough money from her share of the profits, maybe
she could get to Los Angeles—where, as a matter of fact,
she wished she were at the moment.

Up until now Lauren had been feeling sorry for the
poor housewives of 1906, but Elizabeth's life-style
changed her thinking somewhat. When dinner was finally announced, it was served by a battery of servants
and Elizabeth wasn't required to do more than lift her
fork to her mouth and partake of the food. Her conversation was also liberally sprinkled with talk of her seam-
stress, her milliner, her cook and her hairdresser. It was
obvious she didn't have to do anything for herself.

When, over dinner, the girls learned that Lauren was
the Lauren, the one who wrote the controversial column
in the newspaper, they were overjoyed.

"I love the way you tell all the women to get a college
education," the older girl said. "I wish you could convince Papa that I should go to university. He thinks it's
unfeminine."

"And I concur with your father," intoned Elizabeth.

Then all eyes turned to Lauren and she was put on the
spot. "I had a college education," she told them.

Glances were exchanged as though agreeing that such
an education must account for her unseemly behavior.

Lauren was thinking of what to say next when she was saved by the younger girl, who began, "And today, when you advised that young man who was too shy to ask the girl out, to be daring, to grab her and kiss her the next time he saw her, I thought that was *marvelous*. Of course he'll probably get slapped for his efforts. I know *I'd* slap him."

She noticed that she had Early's full attention. "I didn't see that column, Lauren."

"That's because you haven't got to that section yet. It's at home."

"I can show it to you now if you'd like," said the younger daughter, but Early told her he could wait.

"Is that how gentlemen behave in France?" asked Elizabeth.

"Sometimes worse," reported Lauren, tired of acting polite.

"But what could be worse?" asked the younger girl.

While everyone waited for her reply, Lauren wished for at least a small quake to draw the attention away from her. "Actually," she said at last, finally backing down, "that advice was meant to be humorous." When no one laughed, she managed to fill her mouth with enough food that answering another question was impossible.

Another hour's worth of conversation was required before they were allowed to leave, but for the most part Lauren kept silent. She was being unfair to Early again, this time making a poor impression on his cousins, which would reflect badly on him.

By the time they left the house she was sure he must be furious with her, but once on the sidewalk he burst out laughing.

"That'll be the last invitation we get from them for a good while, I should think."

"Sorry about that," she murmured contritely.

"Don't be sorry, they bore me to death. The girls are all right, but give them a few years and they'll be just like Elizabeth."

Lauren smiled. "And here I was thinking you were showing me Elizabeth so I'd have a prototype to model myself on."

"Heaven forbid! I'd suffocate with a woman like that around all the time."

"It would probably aid your blood pressure, though."

"You're wrong, Lauren. I can't tolerate women who talk about nothing but clothes, who don't have the faintest idea what's happening in the world. Why do you think I've stayed single so long?"

"But surely there must be some women—"

"Oh, there are some, to be sure. But they're usually bluestockings, and for the most part I find them singularly unappealing."

"Cindi and I talk about clothes," she reminded him.

"Certainly, but not all the time."

Lauren thought a change of subject was in order and managed to get Early onto the topic of horse racing the rest of the way home. It was not uncommon for Early to spend an afternoon at the track.

When they got inside the house, Lauren started for the stairs, but Early stopped her. Without any warning, he put his hands on her shoulders and tilted his head down toward hers.

"What are you doing, Early?"

His eyes gleamed. "I was attempting to kiss you."

"Aren't you rushing things a little?"

"Well, Lauren, I was only taking that advice you gave to the young man."

"That was a joke, Early!"

"I think not." Again his head bent toward hers, but she twisted away from him.

"Early, please—don't start something now."

"Don't ask me to wait until 1987, Lauren. I'll be dead by then."

She went back to him and put her hands on his arms. Then, standing on tiptoe, she brushed his lips with her own. "Good night, Early, and thank you." Before he could respond, she turned and ran up the stairs.

Cindi was in bed reading one of the books she'd found in Early's study. "How'd it go?" she asked.

"Dreadfully. I'm not fit to take out in proper company, I'll tell you that."

"Don't worry, if things go well we'll be able to form our own group, where we're not looked upon as freaks."

Lauren undressed and sat down on her mattress. "I just hope we get some people who know something. Like how to invent television, for starters."

"Or at the very least a hair dryer."

"I have a hair dryer," said Lauren. "It's just that I can't find any electrical outlets. What we could use is an electrician."

"And a plumber."

"Or maybe a rock star who could entertain us."

"Or an astronaut. Wouldn't that amaze Early?"

"Or someone who builds computers." Lauren sounded wistful.

They kept going until they ran out of ideas. But it didn't matter, because in the end, all they got was Kevin.

Chapter Nine

A man of indomitable energy and push can obtain lucrative employment by calling on F. Parson, rooms 44-45, 330 Pine Street.

AFTER ALL THE WAITING, the endless speculation, Kevin Cunningham showed up on their doorstep one morning shortly after Early had left for work.

Lauren had answered the knock, thinking it might be the mail. Unbeknownst to Early, she had queried the Los Angeles newspapers by letter, asking if they'd be interested in running a local version of her "Dear Lauren" column. It would be nice if she already had a job when she arrived in the Southern California city.

She wasn't even thinking about someone responding to their posters. She had about given up on that.

Lauren looked out the door, squinting in the bright sunlight and feeling a little disappointed it wasn't the mailman. Standing on the front porch was a blond, bearded giant grinning down at her. "May I help you?" she asked him, almost wondering if he could be.... But he was wearing 1906 clothes. Ill-fitting, perhaps, but nonetheless authentic.

"First I didn't believe it when I saw the picture, you know, the TV set, and now I can't believe what I'm seeing in person." He held out a large hand with a lot of blond hair on the back. "I'm Kevin Cunningham, and I'm damn glad to see a pair of jeans survived the time change."

"*You*? You're *really* . . . ?" She found herself hanging on to his hand, not wanting to let go.

"You got it! One of Miss Piggy's fans in person." He couldn't seem to take his eyes off her.

With one motion, Lauren released his hand and turned back into the house. She shouted, "Cindi, get down here!" then turned back to Kevin and grabbed him by the arm. "God, we'd about given up! Come in, come in— welcome to the halfway house."

Cindi was racing down the stairs, then paused at the bottom to better assess the stranger. "Is he . . . ?" she asked, her face full of hope.

"Absolutely," Lauren told her, propelling Kevin forward so Cindi could get a good look at him. "You see before you one of Miss Piggy's greatest fans."

Cindi let out a war whoop, running up to Kevin and giving him a bear hug, only he was so much taller that the hug was around his waist. "I'll get the champagne," she said, taking off for the kitchen. "Don't say anything until I get back," she shouted.

Kevin's face was almost splitting with his grin. "You really know how to make a guy feel welcome."

"We've had that champagne on ice for days," Lauren chided him good-naturedly. "What took you so long?"

"I've been out of town. I got a construction job over in Oakland and just got back last night. When I saw the poster nailed to the side of my rooming house I thought I was seeing things. You know what it meant to see a picture of a TV screen? When I finally realized that what I was seeing was true, I swear to God I did a song and a dance right there in the street. Then I couldn't wait to get over here and check it out. I've been up since about five this morning just waiting till I thought it was a reasonable hour to come by.''

"Cindi drew that—the TV screen. We figured anyone would recognize it. You know, any one of us."

"She's good, yeah, I recognized it right away. A TV screen in 1906—it blew my mind!"

Cindi appeared with the champagne. "You started talking without me," she protested, but she didn't really seem to mind. "Upstairs or down?"

"I guess down here," suggested Lauren. "Kevin looks too big for that furniture upstairs."

For a while they simply sat around drinking champagne, killing off the bottle with toast after toast. Then Lauren asked Kevin, "It did happen to you during the earthquake, right?"

He nodded. "Yeah, and it couldn't've hit at a worse time as far as I was concerned. I was jogging in Golden State Park and when I came to, there I was, in shorts and a tank top, looking for all the world like a sexual pervert." He grinned. "Yeah, okay, it sounds funny now, I can dig it, but at the time..."

"What'd you do?" asked Cindi, practically convulsed in laughter.

"Well, it took me a while to figure out something drastic had changed. I knew there'd been an earthquake and I knew I'd been knocked out by something, but I felt all right when I came to, so I got back up and started jogging again. It didn't take me long to figure out the scenery had changed and that there were a lot of strange-looking people in the park, but even then I didn't think it was me who was strange, you know what I mean?''

Cindi and Lauren nodded.

"Then, along about the time I was realizing something *really* was wrong, these cops stopped me and kind of politely asked what I was doing outdoors in my un-dergarments—that's what they call 'em, you know. So I'm not really sure what the beef is about, but I see these guys mean business and they don't look like cops are supposed to look, you know? And there's this crowd gathered around and all these people are dressed like the dark ages except for me, so I think, okay, you're dreaming, Kevin. It's one of those dreams like you had when you were a kid and suddenly you were in school, only you were still wearing your pajamas and everyone is staring at you. So I think, okay, I'll go along with the dream. Just joking at that point, you know? So I say a bunch of men just robbed me and took all my money and my clothes, then hit me over the head with something. And I had the bump on my head to prove it.''

"Did they let you go?'' Lauren asked.

"What happened, first they bundled me off into this cop car, only it wasn't like any cop car I've ever seen. It had *horses* pulling it. And I'm still thinking it's a dream until I get a good whiff of the horses and almost step in something in the street. I was thinking this wasn't like any dream I'd ever had—something was really wrong or else the bump on my head had made me bonkers. So these guys take me down to the station and ask me all these questions and make me swear out a warrant for the robbers. I give them my real address, and I guess that was okay, and then they loaned me some clothes to go home in." He tugged at the front of his shirt. "These are the clothes. Anyway, I walked home, and I knew deep down all the time I was walking that something wasn't kosher, but it wasn't until I got home and saw that my building wasn't even there that I started to understand. Well, understand isn't the right word. I guess you two know what I mean."

"I had to go out and *steal* clothes," Lauren told him.

"Well, you do what you have to do to survive," reflected Kevin. "I've got to admit that at one point I figured I was *on* something."

"Me, too," said Cindi.

"I figured this friend of mine had liberally laced the brownies," said Lauren, and they all laughed. "Do you have any theories on why we're here? In 1906?"

Kevin shook his head. "Doesn't make any sense to me, except maybe the business about the two quakes."

Lauren and Cindi exchanged glances.

"You do remember the 1906 quake, don't you?" he asked them.

"I hadn't, but Cindi reminded me," Lauren admitted. "She has this theory that we're going to be sent back to 1987 when it hits."

He looked at Cindi. "You know something *I* don't?"

"No, it's just a feeling I have. But it makes more sense than anything else."

"Do you have any idea how bad the '87 quake was?" Lauren asked him.

"No, I wish I did. I left a wife and kid back there somewhere."

"Oh, no," cried Lauren, wondering how she'd feel if she were in that position.

"Then you must *really* want to go back," said Cindi.

In moments his expression had changed from good-natured to tragic. "If they survived—and I gotta believe they did—I guess I was just considered one of the casualties. One of those who disappeared."

"I was at a McDonald's and people in cars were just swallowed up," recalled Lauren, then thought maybe she shouldn't have said that. The same thing could have happened to his family.

Cindi got up. "I think we need some more booze. Be right back."

Kevin looked at Lauren and grinned. "Listen, I didn't mean to put a damper on things—"

"A *damper*! You lost a wife and child and you're worried about *us*?"

"That other part, it doesn't seem real. Oh, hell, none of it seems real. But I've got to believe they're okay. Our building was supposedly earthquake-proof, so maybe they are. But listen, I'm so happy to know I'm not the only one, that you two are here. It was really lonely, you know?"

Lauren nodded, then remembered something. "You were the one in the Adidas, weren't you?"

"How'd you know about my Adidas?"

"That's when I knew I wasn't the only one. I was walking around the Union Square area one day when I saw these Adidas ahead of me, but by the time it dawned on me what that meant, you had disappeared. I searched for you for hours. But that's how Cindi and I got together, because I put this personal ad in the paper."

"I haven't been reading the papers."

Cindi came back in and poured them all more champagne. "He's the one in the Adidas?"

Kevin pulled up one of his pant legs, which were hanging over his shoes, and lifted his foot. "I'm still wearing them. In fact I'm still wearing my running shorts and tank top for underwear, but I imagine you can live without seeing them."

Cindi laughed, but Lauren was staring at his shoes. "Did you dye them?"

"No, they just got dirty doing construction work."

"But the ones I saw were red with white stripes."

"Mine have always been navy," commented Kevin, then realized what that meant. "So there's more of us out there, is that it? Hell, you know what we could do? We could buy an island somewhere and start our own colony of 1987ers or whatever you'd call us."

"Well, whoever he is, it's thanks to him—or her—that the three of us have found each other," said Lauren.

"I guess we gave up hope too soon," conceded Cindi. "We've got to put up more posters and more ads in the paper."

Lauren was nodding, then she asked Kevin, "You don't happen to be an electrician, do you?"

"I wish I were, believe me. What you see before you is a high school math teacher. The only thing I know about electricity is how to change a light bulb. But I'm good with my hands and I figure after the earthquake I'm going to be able to get all the carpentry work I want. You women planning on sticking around for the next one?''

Lauren looked over at Cindi. "Cindi thinks she's going back, so she's staying. I'm planning on moving to L.A. I don't feel like having that experience twice—at least not twice in one year.''

"Sorry to hear that," said Kevin. "Now that I've found you, I kind of hate to think of your leaving that soon.''

"It's not until summer, is it?'' Cindi asked him.

"Far as I know it's in April sometime.''

Lauren looked at Cindi, a horrified expression on her face. "You said summer.''

"I thought it was.''

"It was April," Kevin informed them. "I don't know the exact date, but I think we could find out.''

"How?'' they both demanded.

"You know who Caruso was?''

They nodded.

"Well, if I remember correctly, he was singing here the night before the quake. When they start advertising his concert or the opera he was appearing in, then I guess it's time to prepare. I don't think more than a few hundred people were killed, though, Lauren. Most of the damage was from the city burning down, not the quake.''

That news did nothing to reassure Lauren, who was far more afraid of fires than earthquakes. "Kevin, is there any way this house could be made safe? Like fireproof?''

"How'd you two get this house, anyway?''

"It's not ours," Lauren explained. "It belongs to a reporter on the *Chronicle*, Early Cruz. He's been great, really great, even though I'm convinced he thinks we're crazy. Listen, you want to stay here if it's all right with Early?"

Kevin looked doubtful. "Hey, that's not necessary. I've got a room and a little money I've earned."

"I had a place too," Cindi told him, "but it's not the same. Here we don't have to watch everything we say or do."

"There's plenty of room," Lauren assured him. "Of course I'll have to get Early's permission, but I'm sure I can get it."

"Early's going to let you have whatever you want," teased Cindi, smiling.

Kevin started grinning. "He your boyfriend?"

"I don't want to get into that," said Lauren. "Suffice it to say, he's about a hundred years too old for me."

Kevin stretched out his arms. "Well, if it's okay with this Early, yeah, it'd be a kick. You're the first people I've had to really talk to."

"What about the house?" asked Lauren again.

"This is wood, right? One of those Victorian ones?" She nodded.

He shook his head. "No way. I'd bet anything this is one of the ones that go in the fire. A fire the size of that one, there's nothing you can do."

"I know one thing he can do," said Lauren. "Sell it. We've got to convince him to sell it quick and get another one out of town."

"He won't do it," Cindi told her.

"I know."

"You could pick up property in Sausalito real cheap," suggested Kevin. "You know what that goes for in '87?"

"It's cheap," observed Cindi, "because there's no bridge going over there."

"Still, we ought to talk to him about it," persisted Kevin. "Maybe he'll listen to me. I could help him build a new house, kind of repay him for letting us stay here."

"I could do the interior design," offered Lauren. "We could build the first modern house in San Francisco. Wouldn't that be a kick?"

"It could be the first house with multiple bathrooms," joked Cindi, and they all laughed.

Lauren got up. "Come on, I want to show you the third floor," she said, and they all went upstairs. While they were up there, Cindi started designing a house on paper and they both gave her suggestions.

"The only thing is," admitted Kevin, "I kind of like all this old stuff. My wife and I collected antiques."

Lauren and Cindi stared at him as if he'd gone off his rocker.

"You're going to get along just *fine* with Early" was Lauren's only comment.

BY THE TIME Early got home a feast was spread out on the table. Cindi had gone to Chinatown to do some food shopping and had prepared several Chinese dishes. Kevin had baked a respectable-looking chocolate cake from scratch, so respectable looking, in fact, that Cindi and Lauren had agreed he wouldn't make a bad husband. Lauren had supplied several bottles of wine and had even set the table with the good china that had belonged to Early's mother. To get Early mellow was the order of the day.

They were all in the kitchen when they heard him arrive, and Lauren told them to stay out of sight until she broke the news to him.

Early came down the hall and peered into the dining room. "What's the occasion?" he asked.

Lauren smiled sweetly. "We have company for dinner."

He grunted. "*More* of you showed up?" As though she were pulling them out of hats, thought Lauren.

"Yes, this morning. His name's Kevin Cunningham."

"I was beginning to think it was an all-female venture. This one's a man, though?"

"Yes. I think you'll like him, Early."

Early didn't seem so sure, but he sat down at the head of the table and Lauren called for the others to join them.

Kevin said, "Nice to meet you, sir," when introduced, even though he was only about three years younger than Early, but Early seemed to appreciate the fact that one of them at least had some manners.

"Been cooking again, I see," he remarked to Cindi as he helped himself to ample portions of the food. They'd been amazed to learn that Early had never eaten Chinese food before Cindi moved in.

No one spoke much. They were all waiting to see what Early would say. He ate in silence for a while, obviously enjoying the meal, then said to Kevin, "So you're another survivor of that infamous earthquake, are you?"

Kevin looked amused. "I'm afraid so."

Early smiled all around. "You have the same tale to tell as the women?"

Kevin nodded. "Essentially the same. I don't have any explanation for it, if that's what you mean."

"Kevin had a wife and child," Lauren put in, thinking that might make him more palatable to Early, especially as a houseguest.

"Sorry to hear that," said Early. "You have my sympathy."

"Thank you. I just have to keep believing they're all right."

Early cocked an eyebrow at Lauren, but directed his question to Kevin. "What about this 1906 earthquake I've been hearing about. You know anything about that?"

"Of course," replied Kevin. "And to the best of my recollection, it occurs in April."

Early started to smile. "So, the date's been moved up. Last I heard it was sometime in the summer."

"I thought it was summer," admitted Cindi. "I don't know why."

"Actually," said Lauren, "with Kevin's help, I think we can pinpoint it exactly. You know who Caruso was, Early."

"Course I know who he is. Everyone knows who he is."

"Well, the earthquake is supposed to occur the day after Caruso sings here. So we figure if we can find out when that is, then we'll know exactly."

"He'll be coming to town with the Met," Early informed them. "Go to the opera house and ask them the schedule."

"There's only one problem," said Kevin. "He might be singing more than one night."

"As I said," reiterated Early, "go and find out." He sounded as though he thought he had singlehandedly solved their problem. And in a sense, he had.

Lauren decided to bring up something more pressing. Early seemed to be in a good mood and might be open to suggestions. "We were discussing this house," she began, "and we wondered if you'd be interested in selling it."

"You rich?" Early asked Kevin.

"No, sir, we weren't interested in buying it. It's just that the major damage in the quake was from the fires, and I have a feeling this is one of the houses that'll be destroyed for sure."

"I have fire insurance," Early explained.

"Yes," said Lauren, "but if the whole city burns down, do you really think the insurance companies will pay off?"

Early gave a smug smile. "If they want to stay in business they will."

"What we were thinking," Lauren began, "was that maybe you could sell the house quick and buy another one in Sausalito. You wouldn't believe what they get for property over there in the eighties."

"That'll hardly help *me*," Early remarked. "I don't figure on being around in the eighties—unlike some people who think they're going to be whisked forward in time." He shot Cindi a wry look. "You believe that, too?" he asked Kevin.

"No, sir, I don't. I'd like to believe it, but I have a feeling we're stuck here for good."

"Anyway, what you're suggesting is highly unethical. Why should the people I sell the house to get burned down. You think that's fair?"

"No," replied Lauren and Kevin.

"We hadn't thought about that," Cindi admitted.

"You got a job?" Early asked Kevin.

"Yes, in construction. I'm working as a carpenter."

"Is that what you did in your former life?"

Kevin shook his head. "No, I taught high school math."

"Mathematics?"

Kevin nodded.

"I always liked mathematics," Early told him, drawing groans from the two women.

Kevin glanced around the table with a smile. "I was thinking of writing a book on the new math...try to get it published."

"Don't," implored Lauren, who had hated the new math.

"Yeah, I don't think they're ready for that," Cindi agreed.

"I'd be interested in hearing about it," said Early. "You mean along with television and movies and all those other wonders, they also have a different system of mathematics? And here I thought the old one worked fine."

"It's just a new way of getting the answers, a more understandable way," explained Kevin. "I'd be glad to show it to you if you're interested."

Early glanced at Lauren. "Unless you have a poker game in mind for after dinner."

"No, go ahead," said Lauren. "Cindi and I have some sewing to do."

"You play poker?" Early asked Kevin.

"I've played."

"Good. We can use a fourth hand. I'm assuming, of course, that you're staying."

"Well..."

"Can he, Early?" asked Lauren, thinking this had been easier than she'd thought.

"It's all right with me," replied Early. "I was getting a little tired of being surrounded by women anyway. A carpenter, eh? Maybe I could get you to build me some shelves."

"I'd be glad to," said Kevin, "but I'd rather build you a new house in Sausalito."

Early didn't have anything to say to that.

WHEN LAUREN and Cindi came downstairs two hours later dressed in the matching Chinese outfits they'd made from sheets tie-dyed in red and blue, they had to demand an audience. Reluctantly Early glanced up from the math problems Kevin was doing for him at the dining room table.

"Is that an example of what you think you're going to sell to the good women of San Francisco?" Early inquired.

"Just for at-home wear. Don't you like them?"

"Just don't make one for me."

"We thought we'd take another mattress up for Kevin," said Cindi, but Early shook his head.

"Kevin can sleep in my parents' room."

"But there's no mattress in that room anymore," Lauren informed him.

"Then bring one down and you two can double up. I don't know how you did it in 1987, but in 1906 the men are going to occupy one floor and the women another. And I don't want to hear any argument out of you, either, Lauren."

"I wasn't going to argue, Early."

"Good. You're learning."

Lauren set up the table for a poker game and they soon found that Kevin was more than a passable player. He took all their money in short order, inspiring Lauren to teach them all bridge.

When Early excused himself at one point to go to the bathroom, Kevin remarked, "I thought you said he didn't believe you?"

"He doesn't," insisted Lauren.

"Well, he believed *me*. He asked me all kinds of questions and I think he's convinced now."

"Convinced of what?" asked Early, coming into the room.

"Convinced that we're who we say we are."

"Is that true, Early?" Lauren asked him.

"Well, Kevin's pretty convincing. Particularly when he got into quantum physics and nuclear fission and all that."

Lauren was furious. "That really does it, Early!"

"What?"

"We've spent days trying to convince you, but a couple of hours with Kevin and suddenly your doubts vanish. It's because we're just women, right? You'll listen to a man, but not to us."

"He was convincing, that's all."

"That is *not* all! If I'd been a man, you would've believed me from the start, right?"

Early began to smile. "If you had been a man, Lauren, I wouldn't have bought you a drink in that bar in the first place."

"I think you ought to be warned, Early," said Kevin. "Women have a lot of rights in 1987."

"Then aren't we fortunate this is 1906," Early declared, a fatuous smile on his face.

Frustrated and angry, Lauren got up from the table. "Let's go to bed," she said to Cindi.

"Don't forget to bring the mattress down first," Early reminded her.

"Bring it down yourself!"

"Just giving you some of your rights," Early retorted, ducking his head as though he thought she'd throw something at him.

And it took all of Lauren's self-control not to.

"WHAT DO YOU THINK of Kevin, Cindi?" asked Lauren when they were both in bed. They were wearing their new outfits as pajamas, finding them more comfortable than Lauren's nightgowns.

"What amazes me is he's straight. The odds were pretty much against that, you know."

"But don't you like him?"

"Sure I like him. I'd even like him in '87."

"What do you mean?" asked Lauren.

"Well, you do realize, don't you, that we'd probably like anyone who showed up from our time."

"Yeah, I've thought about that. Well, we know there's at least one more out there. We're going to have to step up the campaign."

"You know, Lauren, anyone from 1987 who knew about the 1906 quake is probably long gone by now."

"We've got to do something about *that*, too."

"No one's going to believe us," Cindi said with a sigh. "And even if Early finally does, he's not going to make himself look ridiculous by telling anyone else."

"I know. I've been thinking, Cindi, what we've got to do is think of some way to get everyone out of town that day."

"I could be wrong—we could check on this with Kevin, maybe he knows—but I think it happened when everyone was sleeping. I think that's why the casualties were so low."

"How do you know that?"

"You know that thing down at Fisherman's Wharf where you can take a ride through old San Francisco and experience the earthquake? Kind of like a Disneyland ride?"

Lauren nodded. "I've seen the outside but I never went in."

"I went in once with some friends who were visiting. I only wish I'd paid more attention. But I'm pretty sure the quake happened in the middle of the night."

"We're never going to get people to leave their homes in the middle of the night."

"There's got to be a way," insisted Cindi. "We'll think of one."

"That won't save the city, though. There's nothing we can do about the fires." Lauren extinguished the light and rolled over. "I was surprised the way Early took to Kevin."

"Yeah, *now*. I just hope Kevin doesn't start showing an interest in you, or Early will throw him out."

"He's married, Cindi."

"Not in 1906, he isn't."

"Well, he's all yours. I'm going to L.A. You know what I was thinking?"

"What?"

"When did movies start, Cindi?"

"I have no idea. Pretty soon, though, I'll bet."

"You know what I could do? I could write screenplays of all the movies I've seen. I figure I could become rich and famous."

"I don't think so, Lauren. I think everything has its time. Anyway, the first movies were silent."

"That's even easier—they'd be a cinch to write."

"Well, when I'm back in 1987, I'll go to the nearest film library and look up old movies. If I see your name as a screenwriter, I'll know you made it."

"That gives me an idea," said Lauren. "Listen, if you *do* make it back to 1987, if that really happens, I'll keep a journal for you and put it somewhere where you'll find it, so you'll know what happened after you left. And I'll expect you to get in touch with my parents, of course.''

"Of course,'' agreed Cindi.

"The thing is,'' began Lauren, very serious now, "I want to change history. I really do.''

"Good luck, kid. I hope you make it.''

"I hope you make it, too. Back, I mean. Of course if you do, then I'll wish I'd taken you more seriously.''

"It wouldn't hurt to try.''

"You knew where you were, Cindi, but I'd never be able to find that McDonald's again.''

"I'll make you a promise, Lauren. If I do get back, I'll boycott McDonald's for the rest of my life.''

"You said you never ate there anyway.''

"So it'll be an easy promise to keep.''

Chapter Ten

Earthquake Shock Felt in Missouri and Kansas

KANSAS CITY, Jan. 7—A slight earthquake shock was felt in the city at about 6:17 this morning. No one is thought to be dead as a result, but property damage...

LAUREN HAD OFTEN WONDERED what she would do with the time remaining to her if she found out she had, say, six months to live, or if the world was supposed to come to an end at a specific date. Now she knew.

Despite the fact that Cindi was certain she was going to be transported back (or forward) to 1987 sometime in April, and despite the fact that Lauren was planning to move to Los Angeles around the same time, the two of them had almost boundless energy in the weeks prior to that anticipated event in April.

There was no sense at all in simply sitting around and waiting for what was sure to come. They started project after project, keeping busier than they'd ever been in their former lives.

Of course Cindi had no preparations to make for her journey. She thought she merely had to be in the right place at the right time and by some miracle she'd be back in '87. Lauren, on the other hand, was preparing for her move to L.A. The newspapers she had written to for a job hadn't answered, but she wasn't going to let that deter

her. She cut out her columns as they appeared each day
and made a portfolio of them. She was sure that when she
showed up in Los Angeles some newspaper would take
her on. If not with the "Dear Lauren" column, then
she'd think of something else.

For someone who wasn't planning on being around in
1906 much longer, Cindi was determined to change the
fashions of the day. She had sewn and Lauren had dyed
about two dozen Chinese outfits before they ran the ad
in the *Chronicle*:

Ladies!

The Latest in At-Home Wear from Paris

We have a limited number of Oriental Lounging Pajamas, the outfit that is currently the rage on the Continent. For those ladies who act quickly, sets may be had
for the low price of only $1.50.

When no orders came pouring in, Lauren and Cindi
took to wearing the outfits around the house, and Lauren was going to take them to L.A. with her. She didn't
know what L.A. was like in 1906, but she did know that
in general Southern Californians weren't as conservative
as Northern Californians, and she thought maybe their
designs would go over better in the warmer, more relaxed climate of the south.

Cindi didn't give up, though; indeed, she was just
starting. "If we can't get them into pants," she told
Lauren, "we could at least modify what's being worn, try
to make it more comfortable. Do you know these women

are still wearing impossible corsets? That lace up? I don't see how they breathe, let alone wear them all day.''

She made a number of drawings of the way she'd like to change the current mode of dress. She shortened the skirts, but not too much, dispensed with the petticoats and gave the dresses a looser-fitting look over all.

When Lauren saw them she remarked, ''Yes, that's an improvement, but I don't think we're going to convince the ladies.''

''I don't see why not,'' Cindi disagreed, pointing out several refinements Lauren hadn't noticed.

''Mostly because these dresses aren't going to look as pretty. Uncomfortable as they may be, Cindi, you have to admit the clothes these days *look* good. In fact I'd say they're one of the prettiest fashions of all time. And the hairdos—they've got to be a real pain to do, but I haven't seen any woman they haven't flattered.''

''What about the bathing suits?'' suggested Cindi. ''We could at least improve upon those.''

''Yes, but our improvements would make people think they'd be going around stark naked. I'm not saying something can't be done, but we've got to take it slower.''

''I've only got a few weeks,'' grumbled Cindi.

''I was thinking,'' said Lauren. ''You know what might work? How about culottes? They'd still look like long skirts, but they'd be easier to get around in. And we could make them a little shorter.''

Even as Lauren was describing them, Cindi was sketching them out. ''Yeah, look at this, Lauren. Why don't we convert some of those skirts of Early's mother. We could wear them around, let them be seen.''

"We could show them to the stores, see if they wanted to buy some," Lauren added.

"Yeah, I think people might be receptive to these. And if we can get women to go for culottes, Lauren, next we can go into actual pants."

Designing clothes was all for fun, though, just to pass the time. Their real project was to warn the city of the imminent earthquake, and in this they were helped by Kevin and, to a lesser degree, by Early.

Kevin still worked during the day, having no problem finding jobs doing carpentry. But at night and on Sundays, and on the few days he wasn't able to get work, he and the women spent all their time trying to find the best ways to warn the people, prepare them and, if possible, lessen the effect the earthquake would have on the city.

It was Kevin's suggestion that they make a list of things each individual should have on hand in case of an earthquake. All of them were native Californians and knew that the most important thing would be a supply of water for drinking purposes, so that topped the list. Food came next, but nothing that was perishable. Thousands of people were going to be left homeless, so they added a ground covering of canvas and blankets to the list.

"Better put whiskey on that list, too," said Early. But Lauren admonished, "The last thing we want, Early, is a lot of drunks wandering the streets."

"First-aid supplies," suggested Cindi, and Kevin wrote it down.

"And money," added Lauren. "If the banks are hit, people are going to wish they had their money at home."

"And their insurance policies," joked Early.

The list finally met their satisfaction, and they added a warning at the bottom that each household should have these supplies kept in one place in case an earthquake struck and they had to flee quickly.

"I think I could get that printed in the newspaper," offered Early, which surprised Cindi and Lauren. They had wanted to do a fashion column for the newspaper, but Early had said "Dear Lauren" was quite enough of a contribution from the aliens.

"That'd be great, Early," said Kevin.

"Well," Early went on to explain, "we had a couple of quakes back in '65 and '68, and the one in '68 was pretty bad. I don't think it would appear too unusual if people in this area were kept prepared. Everyone knows it could happen again."

"They just don't know how soon," said Lauren.

The paper did run the list, along with an article by Early describing the prior quakes and warning that such a disaster could happen again when people least expected.

"I hope people don't remember this article of mine after the quake happens," Early said. "I don't want to get the reputation that I'm some kind of fortune teller."

"*That's* what I could be," Cindi announced, "a Chinese fortune teller."

"I thought of that a long time ago," said Lauren, "but I don't think people want to hear about earthquakes and who's going to be the next president. They want to hear if they're going to be rich and successful in love, that kind of stuff."

"I could do a column," continued Cindi, undeterred. She was always trying to think up ideas for columns.

"Like that psychic in D.C., the one who's always predicting things."

"Forget it," said Early.

"I don't think it's such a bad idea," Kevin disagreed. "The three of us ought to be able to come up with enough events we remember. The war, for sure."

"If these things were meant to be predicted," Early argued, "we would've been sent a prophet."

"Maybe we *are* prophets," Cindi suggested, but everyone laughed at her and she gave up the thought.

In addition to the list and article in the newspaper, Early had several thousand copies of the list printed up at the paper at his own expense, and they spent the last two weeks in February canvasing the city and putting notices in the mailboxes of every building. Cindi was disturbed that she didn't know Chinese and thus couldn't reach everyone in Chinatown, but they figured there were enough people who could read English and hoped the word would be spread.

Actually, they were worried more about the fires that would result from the shocks than the earthquake itself. Kevin wanted to personally inspect all the fire stations, but Early told him he'd be wasting his time.

"First of all, if you start talking about the quake, people are going to justifiably think you're crazy. Secondly, there just isn't any way the city is going to be equipped to handle that many fires no matter how they might start to prepare now. If what you say is true, then there's nothing we can do to prevent the city from burning down."

"At least we can try to get a lot of the people out of here in time," insisted Lauren.

"I had an idea about that," said Kevin. "Do you remember when they used to advertise for, say, street cleaners, and thousands of people would turn up for the job?"

Lauren and Cindi both nodded.

"Well, if we could think of something like that, something everyone would want and would be willing to go out of the city and stand in line all night to get . . ."

"That's when unemployment was so high," observed Lauren. "I can't think what would get enough people to do it now."

"What we have to do is offer something free," Cindi decided. "Something everyone wants but maybe can't afford."

"Exactly," agreed Kevin. "What do you think, Early? What would people want badly enough to line up all night for?"

"You're forgetting something," said Early. "First you give them a list of what to have in case of an earthquake, now you want them out of town. That means they'll lose everything they have of value."

"Maybe," remarked Lauren, "but it's better than losing your life."

"Land," said Kevin. "I'll bet that's what people really want. We could offer free homesites over in Oakland, say to the first 500 people."

Early was shaking his head. "This might be 1906, Kevin, but people aren't *that* gullible."

As a group, they all looked at Early and burst out laughing.

"What's so funny?" he asked.

"Well, no offense," said Kevin, "but if *you* can believe that three people have showed up from 1987..." He broke off laughing again.

Early stood up and was about to walk out of the room, but Lauren intercepted him. "We don't think you're foolish, Early, we think it's wonderful you finally believe us. I personally think it shows a remarkable intelligence on your part."

Early wasn't convinced. "Don't try to sweet talk me, Lauren. And I stand by what I said. I don't think you're going to get enough people over to Oakland for some free land offer to make any difference." But he sat down again, albeit helping himself to some more whiskey.

"Then we'll blitz them," said Cindi. "Listen, guys, I think I have it. We'll do the land offer but we'll also do...oh, I don't know, maybe a couple of job offers and free...what do people want, Early? I've got it. How about free electric water heaters? I'll tell you, *I'd* go stand in line all night for one of those. We can think of a whole number of things and advertise them separately in the paper. Even if we only get a few hundred people, it's better than nothing."

"And all these phony offerings are going to appear in the *Chronicle*, I suppose," Early muttered.

"Not if you don't approve," said Kevin, the diplomatic one of the group. "There are other newspapers we can use, and we can also hand out advertisements on street corners."

"If only we could close down the entertainment that night," suggested Lauren. "Caruso's going to be here, and all the shows. And you know none of the people who go see them are going to leave town afterward."

"That's okay," said Cindi. "At least we ought to reach the poor. And they're the ones who are going to need any help they can get."

"So it's settled?" asked Early.

"Well, there are all the details to work out," Lauren told him. "Why?"

"I just thought we could play a game of poker."

"None of this is going to work anyway," said Cindi, "as I keep telling Lauren."

"Why not?" Kevin asked.

"Because, according to all the science fiction I've ever read, you can't change history. That means, in case you can't figure it out for yourselves, the same number of people are going to be killed and the same number of people are going to be homeless as before, no matter what we do."

"I don't believe that," said Kevin.

"Well, Cindi," Lauren proposed, "when you get back to 1987, look at the history books and see if some people avoided the quake by going to Oakland. Or wherever."

"Anyway," Kevin added, "it's, like you say, science fiction, with the emphasis on *fiction*. Nobody really knows, because no one's gone back in time before."

"Maybe they have and we just don't know it," suggested Lauren. "Maybe lots of people have gone back in time, but, like us, they just settle in and no one ever knows about it. Maybe all the inventors were people who already knew about the inventions."

"An interesting—though confusing—theory," commented Early. "Now why don't we play some cards."

MAYBE IT WAS because the house now resembled a commune, or maybe because his feelings toward her had changed—Lauren couldn't be sure. All she knew was that things between her and Early were no longer the same.

When they had lived together alone, when evenings had been spent in deep conversation, Lauren had always felt, even when she was espousing its impossibility, that eventually she and Early would end up together. Maybe married, maybe not married, but together. At times she had even thought it was fate, despite the fact she didn't believe in fate—at least she hadn't until that day at McDonald's.

Now, however, she and Early were rarely alone together, and when they were it was only for minutes at a time. She found she missed the time they used to spend together. She was crazy about Kevin and Cindi, and the three of them had fast become close friends, but sometimes she yearned for more than friendship.

She had, for a while, considered Kevin as a prospect. It was only natural, since he was the only man she knew from her own time. But Kevin considered himself still married; he probably always would. He'd admitted as much to them on several occasions. He said it didn't do any good telling himself he'd never see his wife and child again, that he'd have to eventually forget them, because in his head, and in his heart, he still thought of himself as part of that family unit.

And, when she was being honest with herself, Lauren had to admit she felt no physical attraction for Kevin. Her feelings toward him were brotherly, not sexual. Now Early, on the other hand, continually stirred her emotions. Forget that he was far too old for her, forget that they had nothing in common, even forget that she was moving to Los Angeles and would no doubt never see him again. Forget all that, and she knew she was only a hair's breadth away from being in love with him.

Things came to a head one evening over an entirely innocent incident. Cindi was out, down in Chinatown distributing leaflets and talking to people about what they could do to prepare for an earthquake. Lauren and Kevin had been on the third floor making up ads for the paper—the free land ads—when Kevin started talking about his wife.

He took Lauren on a sentimental journey back to the time when he had first met his wife. They'd moved in together almost instantly, and he described their wedding, when she was seven months' pregnant with their son. In the middle of telling her about the silly fight they'd had the day before the earthquake, Kevin broke down and cried.

Lauren, who had never even *seen* a man cry before, was at a loss for what to do. If it had been Cindi she would have hugged her, comforted her. Devastated by the agony he was going through, she finally moved over to him and knelt in front of his chair, reaching up and pulling his head down to hers.

Time and Again

"I know, I know," she murmured, hugging him close, knowing she really didn't know, she *couldn't* know what he was going through.

She had no idea how long she held him, but finally the heaving subsided. She rocked back on her heels, then took the sleeve of her blouse and wiped the tears off his face.

"I don't know what happened there," said Kevin, looking mortified.

"It's normal, Kevin. I'm surprised you haven't broken down before this. Don't you think we've all cried at some time or another since we've been here?"

"Yeah, but I'm supposed to be a man . . ."

"Nonsense. You're supposed to be human."

"Thanks, Lauren. You're really something, you know that?" And then he had leaned toward her and kissed her.

She kissed him back the way she'd kiss any friend, meaning nothing by it, knowing it was the same for him. Neither of them heard Early on the stairs.

Kevin was the first to notice him, and he immediately moved away from Lauren. She turned around to see what had attracted his attention—just in time to see Early's back racing down the stairs.

"Oh, God, I really screwed up *this* time, didn't I?" Kevin groaned, distraught once again.

"Don't be silly, Kevin," she insisted, but she knew very well Early would have put the worst interpretation on what he had seen.

"You better go down and talk to him, Lauren."

"I think I'll let him cool off."

"Naw, go on. The guy's in love with you, you know."

"Give me a break, Kevin."

"You know it, don't kid yourself. You could do a lot worse, Lauren. A lot worse. He's a damn good man."

"I know. If only..."

"Forget the damn age thing. As far as we're concerned, we're now of this time period, too. What're you afraid of, some lightning bolt is going to come down and strike you if you have sex with some guy from the past?"

"I don't know. It just seems weird, that's all."

"Hell, I've seen weirder things. Go on, for me if not for you. I don't want him to think I was making a move on his woman."

"I'm not his woman, Kevin."

"I'm telling you, Lauren, if you don't go down this minute, I'm going to start crying again."

That made her smile. "Okay, but if you don't hear from me in an hour, come to my rescue."

She found Early in his study, seated at his desk. His back was to her and she said, "Early? Can we talk?"

"There's nothing to talk about, Lauren. I guess it was bound to happen."

"What was bound to happen? And will you turn around at least?"

He moved the chair around so she could see him, and she was disturbed by his appearance. He looked older, drawn, as though he'd been through a terrible experience. "Come on, Early, what was bound to happen?"

"You and Kevin. It's only natural that when you found someone like yourself..."

"You've got it all wrong, Early. I knew you did. Kevin and I are just friends, that's all. Like you and Cindi are friends."

"There's a difference. I don't kiss Cindi."

"Well, you're different, that's all. We're used to kissing our friends, it's no big deal."

His eyebrows shot up. "Are you telling me, Lauren, that in 1987 you run around kissing men and it doesn't mean a thing?"

"I'm saying it's no big deal. I've probably kissed a couple of hundred men in my life, and very few of them meant anything."

Early appeared disconcerted by her words. "If kissing a man doesn't mean anything, what does?"

"Come on, Early, you don't want to hear about my sex life." She immediately regretted her words when she saw Early's reaction. He looked positively apoplectic.

"Whoa. Just hold on a minute here. As I recall, and correct me if I'm wrong, the night I tried to kiss you, you said for me to slow down. Am I right?"

Lauren nodded, afraid of what was coming.

"And now you're telling me there were men in the past who didn't get that kind of warning from you?"

"It was a different time, Early."

"Just answer the question."

"Early, let's have a drink and talk about this."

"I never thought I'd have to ask you, but are you a virgin, Lauren?"

"Of course I'm not a virgin. I'm over thirty, for God's sake."

With a look of infinite sadness, Early turned back around in his chair, shoulders bent, the picture of dejection.

Lauren walked into the room and closed the door behind her. There had to be something she could say to him to make things right.

"Early, listen to me."

"Go away." His voice sounded anguished.

"No, I'm not going away until we talk this out." She waited, but he didn't tell her to leave again. "First of all, I'm not going to apologize for what you saw upstairs. Kevin had been telling me about his wife, and then he started crying. I felt so bad for him, you would've too, and I took him in my arms and tried to comfort him. That kiss you saw, Early, was merely his way of thanking me for being there. That's all it meant. In fact he was the one who told me to come down here and straighten out the misunderstanding with you."

There was silence for a moment, then Early said, "I guess we don't show affection like that."

"I know you don't, which is why I told you to take it slow that night. That was for you, Early, not me. I probably would've jumped in bed with you *any*time, but—"

"You *what*?"

"Look, there was an attraction from the start. We both felt it. But I knew you took such things more seriously. I thought you'd think I was some...some lady of the night or something if I had sex with you that soon."

Any anguish there had been in his eyes was now replaced by a speculative gleam. "Let me make something clear to you, Lauren. We may have a different system of courting than you had, but in all the essentials we're exactly the same. I may have acted the gentleman with you, but that doesn't mean I wasn't having a good many ungentlemanly feelings.''

She moved over to his desk and sat down on the floor in front of him. ''The thing is, Early, and I've given this a lot of thought, I don't see much point in starting anything now. Sure, we could go to bed, have some fun, but the bottom line is I'm going to Los Angeles and I don't imagine I'll ever see you again.''

''You're staying here with me.''

She shook her head. ''No, I'm not. I've told you before, I'm not going through another earthquake. Wait'll you go through this one, you'll know what I'm talking about.''

''I had thoughts of marrying you. You're the first woman I've ever had those kind of feelings about.''

''I've considered it, too.''

''Of course that's when I thought you were pure.''

''Damn it, Early, you're asking too much! What do you care what I did before I even knew you? Are you telling me you didn't have women?''

''That's different. I'm a man.''

''Well, that kind of thinking doesn't cut any ice in 1987, believe it or not. The women are no different than the men. There is one difference, though, Early—when I had sex with a man, it meant something. And that something, in my case at least, was love.''

''How many times have you been in love, Lauren?''

''Very funny! In other words, how many men have I had sex with?''

Early shrugged.

"All right, Early, if you really want to know, there've been three—and don't look so shocked, okay? Believe me, at my age that isn't very many. In fact, some people would consider me a prude. I'm talking about *real* sex now, not fooling around. Well, wait a minute, to be absolutely accurate I'd have to say four. But the fourth was a mistake. I didn't think it was going to be a mistake at the time, but it turned out to be. It only lasted a couple of weeks. But the others, Early—they were serious. Each time I was in love, each relationship lasted a long time— the longest four and a half years—and each time it might have ended in marriage, except I kept shying away. And I'm glad now I did, because I'd rather be in my position than Kevin's. And I'm not apologizing for my past, Early. I'm explaining. I'm a normal woman and I like to have a man in my life and I also like sex. Now if that makes me some kind of scarlet woman to you, well, I can't help it."

All he said was "Did people stay married in your day?"

"Some of them. There were a lot of divorces, but some marriages lasted. My parents have been married for over thirty years and they're still in love."

"Did you live with these men or what?"

"One I did. The one that lasted four and a half years."

"What happened?"

"He was a musician, but not very successful, and it ate at him. He knew he was good, but just couldn't get the breaks. So, to make a long story short, he got pretty heavily into drugs, and one night I'd had it and threw him out." She saw his questioning look and elaborated, "Like opium, you know, only mostly not as strong. Anyway, that night I found out he'd taken some of my money and bought some coke—one of the drugs—and I couldn't stand it anymore. By then he wasn't the same person anyway. I saw him again just before the quake—before I showed up here. He's about kicked the drugs now, but he's not playing music anymore."

"Did you have sex with him?"

"I told you, I lived with him."

"I mean the last time you saw him."

"Of course not. It was long over."

"I guess I haven't been any angel," Early admitted.

"Oh? You want to list all yours for me?"

"You got all night?"

Lauren leaned forward and rested her arms on his knees. She looked up at him. "Friends, Early?"

"Does that mean we're kissing friends?"

Lauren sighed. "Look, Early, I've got a lot of mixed up feelings about you, but my best guess is that it'd probably be a whole lot smarter if we didn't get involved at this point. I'm leaving and you're not, and I also have a feeling if we did get involved, you'd overly romanticize it. Let's part friends, Early, okay?"

"I wasn't asking for a long speech, Lauren. I just wanted to know if it was all right to kiss you."

She smiled at him. "Of course it's all right." She lifted her face to give him a quick kiss on the mouth, but he had his arms around her before she could back off, and then all she could think about was how did Early, in 1906, learn to *kiss* like that. He was making every guy she'd ever kissed look like a rank amateur, and she was beginning to wonder if 1987 was all she kept insisting it was. She was starting to reassess her thinking about not becoming involved before she left, and then she heard the front door slam.

"Hey, where are you guys?" Cindi was yelling, and with mutual sighs they broke off the kiss.

Chapter Eleven

300 are Killed in Battle With Troops

Russian revolutionists were beaten with heavy loss in a conflict lasting several hours. As word of repression continues in provinces . . .

"I THINK the Russian Revolution is going on," announced Kevin, reading the paper at the breakfast table.

"No kidding?" But Cindi didn't sound particularly interested.

"I didn't think it was this soon," said Lauren.

"You mean what's happening over there is serious? No one told me that," Early groused.

"All I know about it is what I saw in *Reds*," Lauren admitted. "And I was more interested in the love story than the politics."

"Yeah," Cindi agreed. "Warren Beatty wasn't bad."

"Will somebody please tell me about the revolution?" Early requested.

Kevin put down the paper. "It's when the Russians become communists."

"I thought that's what *we* were," said Early. "Isn't this communal living?"

"Well," observed Kevin, "there's communal living and then there's communal living. Hey, let's start a communist revolution here."

"What for?" asked Lauren.

"Maybe that way no one would drop the bomb." Then, seeing the look Lauren gave him, he retracted his words. "Forget it—bad idea."

"What bomb?" inquired Early.

Kevin grinned. "Didn't the women tell you anything?"

"We told him," Lauren complained, "but he didn't believe us."

"I don't remember," said Early.

"I told you about demonstrating against nukes," Cindi reminded him. "I remember, because you were looking at me the whole time like I was crazy."

"You misinterpreted me, Cindi. I was looking at you in awe."

Lauren loved the way Cindi and Early teased each other. She was sure that any initial prejudice Early might have had against the Chinese had been quickly dispelled by Cindi.

"Forget the Russians," said Kevin, "we've got our own problems. It's almost April and we still don't know when the earthquake's hitting."

Cindi glanced over at him. "They told me at the opera house that they'd have the Met's schedule by the end of the month. I guess I'd better check back with them."

"I guess you'd better," Kevin chided lightly.

"I was thinking, Kevin," said Lauren.

"Yeah?"

"Do you really want to be a carpenter the rest of your life?"

"I don't mind. Actually I like it better than teaching high school kids. I get more respect, for one thing."

"It just seems a waste," she said. "I mean, here we are, we have all this knowledge. It seems stupid not to put it to use."

"Yeah, I know," Kevin teased, winking at Early, "you want me to redesign the men's clothes, right? Get them into polyester leisure suits."

"*Please*, not while I'm eating," groaned Cindi.

"I'm serious, Kevin," said Lauren. "Listen, did you ever surf?"

"What's surfing?" asked Early.

"Later, Early," Lauren told him.

"Yeah, I did a little surfing," Kevin told her. "In my youth."

"Could you make a surfboard?"

Kevin was nodding now, starting to smile. "Yeah. Yeah, I see what you mean."

"What?" asked Cindi.

Lauren imparted her idea. "I see no reason why Kevin can't be the one to invent surfing, that's all."

"Yeah," concurred Kevin, enthusiastic now. "I could do it. I could make the boards, no sweat. Who's going to surf, though?"

"Anyone who sees you out there having a good time, I would guess," said Lauren.

"Are you kidding? The water's freezing here."

"I know. I figured maybe you'd like to move down to Southern California when I go."

"You scared to go alone?"

Lauren shrugged. "Not scared, exactly, but it'd sure be nice to have a compatriot along."

"That sounds like fun," said Cindi. "If I weren't going back, I'd join you."

Early didn't say it sounded like fun. In fact he didn't say anything. He just got up and left the table rather abruptly.

"You pissed him off again," said Kevin, shaking his head at Lauren.

"He's welcome to join us if he wants to."

"Hell," said Kevin, "why should he? He's one of the *Chronicle*'s best reporters, he has his house here, his friends, everything. I like San Francisco better than L.A., too."

"If he cared about me, he'd come along."

"You don't ask much of a guy, do you, Lauren? If you cared about him, you'd stay."

"I used to surf when I was a kid," said Lauren, changing the subject. "If I can manage it in today's bathing suits, I'll help you demonstrate. And then I'll fake these letters in my column about people writing in to find out more about surfing. You know—Dear Lauren, My boyfriend spends every Sunday surfing. What should I do?"

Cindi giggled. "And then you write back and say, Join him! Right?"

Lauren laughed. "Right. What do you think, Kevin? I think we could get rich."

"We?"

"Yeah. I'm going to be your partner."

They heard knocking at the front door and Cindi said, "Early locked himself out. Go let him in, Lauren. *Apologize.*"

"For what? What'd I do this time?"

"Come on," pleaded Cindi. "Try thinking of yourself as a houseguest for once. It's a lot easier for everyone when you two are getting along."

"All he has to do is walk around to the back door."

"Lauren!"

"All right, already, I'm going." She stalked to the front door, ready to yell at Early for not taking his key and for walking out on them like that. She yanked open the door, the words already on her tongue, but she didn't get a chance to say anything, because a strange young man shoved right by her into the house.

"If you're looking for Early," she began, but then Early appeared behind her. "What's going on here?" he asked.

"I just thought I'd check the place out," the man was saying, looking around. He gave Lauren the once-over. "Yeah, you got a nice set-up here."

"Go into the kitchen, Lauren, I'll take care of this," Early ordered, but by then Lauren had noticed the man's feet. Or rather what he had on his feet.

"It's *you*," she said, but somehow she didn't feel the same excitement she had when Cindi and Kevin had arrived. There was something about the man she didn't like. Oh, hell, she didn't like *anything* about him. She turned to Early. "He's the one in the Adidas."

"How'd you know about my shoes?" The stranger sounded a little unsure of himself now.

"I saw them in the street one day. Why didn't you answer the ad?"

"*What* ad? I seen your posters. Not bad. Pretty good idea."

"Would you like a cup of coffee?" Lauren asked him, wanting the others to meet him. She knew one thing for sure: she wouldn't have trusted him in 1987. He looked like the kind of guy who thought a good time was hanging around North Beach and mugging gays. Just for laughs.

Early didn't seem happy about her invitation, and he appeared even less happy when the man said he'd prefer something stronger.

Lauren led the way back to the kitchen and the others caught on right away. Kevin was out of his chair and holding out his hand, and the stranger was telling him to call him Rocky.

"Rocky?" said Cindi, almost laughing.

Rocky was obviously annoyed. "Yeah, why not? Listen, I figure I can be anyone I want to be. I mean, does it really matter? Anyway, people always said I looked like him—you know, Stallone."

Lauren couldn't see the resemblance but didn't say so. "Well, Rocky, why don't you sit down and tell us about yourself? What took you so long to come by?"

He slouched over to a chair, spun it around, and sat down on it backward. "What's the rush, huh? We're not going nowhere, are we? I just figured I'd come by, pay my respects, that's all." Lauren handed him the coffee. "Yeah, a little more sugar in that, okay?" he demanded. "The food around here, can you believe it? I mean I used to think I ate bad before."

"Where were you..." began Cindi, and the others chimed in, "...when the earthquake struck."

Rocky took a drink of the coffee, made a face, then said, "You want to hear luck? I'll tell you luck. I just happened to be in police custody when that timely event took place. You might say I lucked out with that one."

"Lucked out?" repeated Kevin. "You mean you like it here? Now?"

Rocky made an expansive gesture with his hands. "Hey, you kidding me? This place is a piece of cake. You know how much I take in on an average day? Go on, take a guess."

"I don't think I want to," said Cindi, exchanging a glance with Lauren.

"Would you mind telling me why you were in police custody?" asked Early.

Rocky shrugged. "Don't lose your cool, man, it wasn't something that's even against the law now. They got me on possession, that's all, not even dealing. I would've beat it, no sweat."

"And what are you doing these days?" Kevin asked him, ignoring Early's perplexed expression.

"I'm making out real good these days. These people—wow—I mean, they don't know from *nothing*. Hey, you got anything to go with this coffee?"

Lauren began to move toward the cupboards, but Early caught her arm. "No, Lauren, he's not to be fed. I want him out of here."

Rocky gave Early an innocent look. "Hey, what's the matter, man? We're all in this together, aren't we? The way I figure it, we could practically take over this city, you dig?"

"Get out," ordered Early, dead serious.

Rocky, a half grin on his face, was eyeing the others for support. He didn't find it.

Early reached down and grabbed Rocky's arm, pulling him to his feet while the chair fell over with a crash. "You want to go out on your own or you need my help?"

Rocky did a little dance, moving around and ducking by Early, then swinging back, his fist moving fast. Early was faster, punching him in the chin so hard Rocky went flying across the room, ending up on the floor against the cupboards.

"You going to get out now?" Early asked him.

Everyone was staring at Early in awe as Rocky rose tentatively to his feet. He managed a last grin. "Yeah, I'm going. I was going anyway. But I'll see you folks around, you know what I mean?"

Early followed him out of the kitchen, while the others stayed behind, silent, until they heard the front door slam and the lock being turned.

"I hope you don't judge all of us by him," said Kevin as soon as Early came back in the kitchen.

Early looked surprised. "Why would I do that?"

"You sure took care of him," said Cindi.

"Yes, very impressive," Lauren agreed. "All it needed was for you to say, 'Make my day.'" She got a chuckle from Cindi, another Clint Eastwood fan.

Early shrugged, but Lauren could see he was pleased. "I used to do a little boxing," he told them.

"I don't think Rocky'll be back," Kevin predicted.

"I think we should report him to the police," said Cindi.

Kevin shook his head. "For what? Being arrested in '87?"

"No, for what he's probably doing *now*."

"Let's just hope the earthquake gets him," suggested Lauren. "And believe me, I never thought I'd say that about a person. And to think I tried so hard to find him. All I can say is, thank God he wasn't the first to show up."

"Well, one good thing," said Cindi.

"What?" asked Lauren, doubtful.

"You won't have to keep wondering anymore about who was wearing those Adidas."

Early sat down and poured himself some coffee. "He's not worth all the time we're wasting on him. I have an idea, why don't we hire a carriage and go to Golden Gate park for the day?"

Kevin exchanged knowing glances with Cindi, then said, "Thanks, Early, but I've got some work to do."

"I was going to go down to Chinatown today," Cindi told them, "talk to the people some more."

Lauren gave Early a rueful look. "I guess it's just you and me, Early."

For some reason, Early didn't seem to mind.

IT WAS THE FIRST TIME Lauren had been to the park since the earthquake. It was a beautiful day, the temperature in the sixties and strollers out en masse. Lauren was wearing a pair of culottes she and Cindi had devised, and she had no trouble keeping up with Early's stride. If Early had noticed she wasn't wearing an ordinary skirt, he didn't mention it.

But then, for the most part, Early was easy to get along with. He never complained that his life had been taken over by three dissidents from 1987 who were always trying to change the way things were in 1906. Sometimes he seemed amused by their schemes, sometimes he joined in, but mostly he seemed merely to tolerate them.

Lauren and Early were only one of a great many couples enjoying an outing in the park. Families were having picnics on the lawns, young men and women were getting acquainted away from the watchful eyes of parents, and in one section Lauren saw a group of boys playing baseball. The only landmark familiar to her was the Japanese Tea Garden, where they sat down to rest for a while.

"What's missing, Early, is runners," she remarked, remembering the Sunday joggers who used to fill the paths of the park. "It was getting so everyone in San Francisco was running."

"You mean people just ran? For no reason?"

"It was supposed to be good for the heart. I always thought the only good to come of the whole running craze was running shoes. Believe me, they're the most comfortable shoes ever invented."

"Do you suppose your friend Rocky runs?" he asked.

"Yeah, from the police. I think maybe we should've done something about him when we had him in the house."

"He wasn't breaking any laws, Lauren."

"Yes, but I've been thinking about it. Have you been reading all those items in the paper lately about women getting their purses snatched?"

He nodded. "You think that's Rocky?"

"I wouldn't be surprised."

"Leave it to the police, Lauren. If it is Rocky, they'll eventually catch him."

"I don't know. With all his knowledge, I'm afraid he'll be able to outsmart the police. I figure I could, if I became a criminal."

Early started to smile. "Now you're going to be a criminal along with all your other ambitions?"

"No, I'm just saying if I wanted to be, I could be a pretty good one. Hijacking, for instance. I bet no one's done any hijacking yet."

His smile faded. "I'm not going to even *ask* what hijacking is."

Laughing, she rose to her feet and grabbed his hand. "Come on, Early—what we need is some exercise. Why don't you try to buy a ball off one of those kids and we'll play some catch?"

"Behave, Lauren," he admonished her, refusing to get to his feet.

"I'm serious, Early. I'm getting out of shape. I can't run in this, but I could catch a ball."

"Why don't you sit down and we—"

"You don't know how to play catch, do you?"

"I've caught a ball or two."

"Yes, but a baseball? Have you?"

Early merely grunted.

"Let's go. I'll give you a few lessons. You're looking at the only girl in the neighborhood who made the Little League team. And don't ask what that is, because I'm tired of explaining everything to you."

The boys were happy to sell them a ball, and Lauren led Early to a more secluded part of the park where she wouldn't cause raised eyebrows among the ladies. Starting close and then, after he got the hang of it, moving farther apart, she and Early tossed the ball back and forth.

Of course Early spent most of his time chasing the ball when he missed, but Lauren thought it was good for him to move around a little. Almost every time she saw him he was sitting down.

When Early finally collapsed in the shade beneath a tree, sweat pouring off his face, Lauren joined him. "You did pretty good for a beginner," she told him.

"I'm sure that's high praise coming from you."

"Now if only there was basketball, we could put a hoop on the outside of the house, in the backyard, and shoot some baskets."

"I can't wait until *that* sport shows up," grumbled Early.

"You'd love it, Early—it's a lot more fun to watch than horse racing."

"The fun isn't in watching the horses run, it's in winning money," he informed her.

Lauren slid down and rested her head in the grass, her legs bent and spread apart beneath the culottes.

"Sit up, Lauren, someone might see you."

"See me what, relaxing?"

"I think the word for you is *rowdy*," he said, but she could see he was trying not to smile.

"Thank you, Early."

"That wasn't a compliment!"

"Hey, Early, since we're all alone together, no one around, why don't you try kissing me again."

"That kind of thing is not done in public, Lauren."

"Oh, come on—no one can see us. You're a good kisser, did I tell you that?"

Early appeared to be sweating again. "No, I can't recall that you did."

"Yeah, well you are. I was surprised."

"Kissing has been going on for hundreds of years. Maybe thousands."

"I guess I was wrong about a lot of things. I thought people in this time didn't like sex—you know, being Victorians and all."

"*Victorians?* That's what we're called?"

"Sure? Didn't you know?"

"I know one thing, Lauren, I think we'd better head back. The way this conversation is going I might be led to attack you in the grass."

Lauren chuckled. "Would that be so terrible?"

"Yes, go on, put on your tough act. But you'd be the first to run."

"Try me, Early."

He got up, brushing off the seat of his pants. "You're incorrigible, do you know that?" He reached down a hand to help her up, then lightly touched her hair with his lips before taking her hand. "Now come on—this 'ghost' is going to take you for a nice stroll through the park, show you how proper ladies conduct themselves on a Sunday afternoon."

"Chicken," muttered Lauren under her breath, but either he didn't hear her or he didn't understand the term.

Once again they were on the path, looking as respectable as the next person, when she said, "Let me have a cigarette, Early."

"I've told you before, not in public."

"Hey, did I ever tell you about Virginia Slims—their advertising?"

"Are Virginia Slims cigarettes?"

She nodded. "Yeah, they were long and thin, much longer than the cigarettes you smoke. Anyway, they had these ads showing women from about this time, I guess, and the women would be hiding and smoking and their husbands would catch them, something like that. The ads showed that not only didn't women *smoke* in the old days, but they had to do what their husbands *said*."

"And rightly so," Early interjected.

"I knew you were going to say that. Anyway, then it would show this really good-looking modern woman, in normal clothes and all—"

"Normal meaning the ridiculous things *you* wear."

"Right. *Normal.* And the slogan was—are you listening?"

"You have my undivided attention, Lauren."

"The slogan was—'You've come a long way, baby!' You get it? You like that?"

Early was nodding, smiling a little. "Yes, I like it. But of course in your case, Lauren, you'd have to reverse the slogan. In your case I'd say, 'You've gone *back* a long way, baby.' Correct?"

Lauren, who always liked to have the last word, couldn't think of a thing to say.

Chapter Twelve

...and on the evening of April 17th, at the Grand Opera House, Enrico Caruso will be singing Don José in Bizet's *Carmen*. The celebrated tenor's appearance is anticipated as the real opening of the season. With Caruso, Madame Olive Fremstad, a Wagnerian soprano, will take the title role for the first time in her career.

"THAT'S IT, THEN," announced Kevin when Cindi came home with the news. "Yes, Caruso in *Carmen* on the seventeenth, that strikes a bell. Which would make the earthquake occur on the eighteenth. Sometime in the early hours of the morning, if I recall correctly."

"I *hope* you recall correctly," said Lauren. "We're kind of depending on it."

"I'm sure of it," Kevin assured her.

"I was hoping it would be toward the end of the month," said Lauren, thinking how little time she had left in San Francisco. They would tell Early when he got home, and she could picture how he would look when he heard the news. His eyes would find hers, not pleading, exactly, but trying to get her to change her mind and stay.

"You're not the type to be frightened," he had said to her once. "Look at how you survived the last one, and that one sent you back in time. You're one of the bravest people I've ever met."

"Once maybe, Early," she had answered him, "not twice. I mean it, I couldn't live through that twice. Anyway, it's not the quake that scares me, it's the fires. Once when I was a kid there was this brush fire coming down from the hills. The schools were closed, and all day my father hosed down the roof, waiting for the fire to hit our neighborhood. It didn't, but it got really close. So close we could see it and feel the heat and even smell it. And we were covered with ashes, all of us. I went up on the roof with my dad and I could see it coming. It was as if we were surrounded by fire for a time. I had nightmares about fires for years after that."

What she didn't say was how much more terrible it must be when a fire consumed a city like San Francisco. In the fire she'd experienced, if the worst had happened they would have got in the car and driven off, leaving the house to burn. But people weren't going to be able to get out of the city so easily. They would be trapped with no way out, some of them in bed. She didn't think avoiding that experience was cowardly; she thought it was the intelligent thing to do.

Early didn't make any attempt to be alone with her those last few days, as though already preparing for the time when she wouldn't be there anymore. She understood; felt the same way. Why continue something that was soon to end? Kevin was working most of the time, even taking jobs at night so that he could get together enough money for the trip to Los Angeles. Lauren and Cindi became inseparable.

"I'm going to miss you," Cindi told her. "When you go through something like this with someone, you really get close."

"I wish you'd change your mind, Cindi."

"I wish you'd change yours. Come with me, Lauren. If we stand in the same spot, hold hands, then I'm sure both of us will go back. It's not like you're staying because of Early. That I could understand."

"I just don't think we have a choice, Cindi. I hope for your sake you're proved right, but I'd give it about a billion to one odds."

"At least you're giving it odds, you're not saying it's impossible."

Lauren smiled. "It would be pretty hard to say that when we both know it can happen. But have you thought what you'll do if you don't get back? Would you consider coming down to L.A.?"

"I don't know, Lauren. I haven't thought that far ahead. Right after the quake I think they're going to need all the help they can get around here, but after that... well, we'll keep in touch, right?"

The week prior to the expected quake, they flooded the San Francisco newspapers with the ads they had made up to lure large numbers of people out of the city on the day in question. They had come up with a wide variety of offers that should appeal to different segments of the population. They could only hope that some people would be willing to wait in line through the night in the expectation of getting something free, and also that they wouldn't find out it was a scam before the earthquake struck.

Without saying anything to Early about it, the three of them made sure he had bottled water on hand and all the other supplies they'd put on the earthquake list. They knew he wasn't planning on staying home that night, that he was going to hang around the *Chronicle* office so that someone was on the scene when the news broke, but in case his house was spared they wanted him to be equipped.

"Why do I feel like I'm deserting a sinking ship?" asked Kevin when they were filling up bottles of water one day.

"Because we are," Lauren replied.

"I feel like I'm deserting all of you," Cindi told them.

"I guess it's called survival," said Kevin, but he didn't sound convinced.

They saw Rocky one more time. He came by the house during the day when only Lauren and Cindi were there. Cindi answered the door and at first was going to slam it in his face, but Lauren came up behind her and said, "I think we ought to warn him."

Rocky heard her and started grinning. "You going to threaten me, girls? Or maybe you think your friend will come to the rescue and punch me out again, is that it?" Then he slid his hand into his pocket and pulled out a knife.

Lauren pushed Cindi aside and stood facing Rocky. "You can put the knife away, Rocky. I only want to help you."

"Yeah, sure you do." But he put the knife out of sight and Lauren felt relieved.

"Do you remember the San Francisco earthquake of 1906?" she asked him, and watched his face change in a way that showed he did.

"Damn. Yeah, I remember hearing about that in school."

"To the best of our belief, it's going to hit on the morning of the eighteenth. So if you want to get out of town before it happens, I suggest you leave now."

But Rocky was nodding his head as though in time to music. "Yeah, listen, that offers possibilities. Yeah, a person could really clean up after something like that."

Lauren realized what a mistake she had made and tried to close the door, but Rocky put his weight against it for a moment while he said, "Hey, I wasn't going to bother you or nothing. And thanks—thanks for the tip."

After he'd gone, Cindi said to Lauren, "I wish you hadn't warned him. Watch, the vulture is going to rob the victims."

"I felt I had to tell him."

"That time, Lauren, I think you shouldn't have gone with your feelings."

On the night of the sixteenth they planned a farewell dinner. Early had been told about it, of course, but he didn't come home as planned. They waited an hour, then finally sat down at the table, and Lauren suddenly wondered what they were celebrating.

Kevin poured them all wine and they started in on the dinner, now cold. "I wonder where we'll all be forty-eight hours from now," he mused, raising his glass to the others.

"We'll be in L.A.," said Lauren, "reading about the quake."

"I wish we could've stuck together," said Cindi, a wistful note in her voice.

"We still can," Lauren told her.

"That's not what I mean. I wish you two were going back with me."

"Believe me," said Kevin, "if I thought it was possible, I would."

"Anything's possible," replied Cindi, but she didn't sound convinced.

Lauren and Kevin were leaving the next morning on the train for Los Angeles. After dinner, the three of them brought down all the furniture Lauren had taken to the attic, with the exception of the mattresses, which they would bring down in the morning. Then they packed their few belongings before having a last drink together.

They were all in bed when Lauren heard Early come home. She rolled over restlessly, and Cindi said, "You ought to go down and say goodbye to him."

"I know."

"Go on, Lauren, you're not going to get another chance. We'll all be around in the morning."

"He told me never to come to his bedroom again."

"He didn't mean to say goodbye."

Lauren lit the lamp, then sat up on the mattress. "Well, at least I'll go dressed this time." She put on her jeans and a sweatshirt. "I'll be back in a few minutes," she told Cindi.

"Take your time."

"Yeah, well, I don't think it's going to take long. I mean, he could've shown up tonight. He knew what we were planning."

"Get serious, Lauren. You're breaking the man's heart and you want him to show up for your farewell? Were you always this way with men?"

"What way?"

"Unfeeling."

"I have just as many feelings as he does, Cindi. Listen, if it's any consolation, I'm in love with the guy."

Cindi sat up. "Then I hope you're going to do more when you go down there than just say goodbye."

"And I think that would be really stupid. It's not going to make me stay, you know."

"Maybe, but it'll give you something to remember."

"What if I don't want to remember?"

She left the room and went down to the second floor. As she passed Kevin's room she heard him snoring, but farther down the hall she could see a light still on in Early's room. The door was partially closed and she pushed it open without knocking. Early, his jacket and tie removed, was standing in front of the wardrobe with his back to her.

"Early?" she said, feeling like an intruder.

He turned around, not saying anything, just watching her, looking, in the shadows, like an old photograph, circa 1906.

And yet in that moment as their eyes met, he'd never seemed more alive to her, and she felt an almost overwhelming rush of emotion for him. She knew she had been playing games with him, punishing him for being of another time, when, all told, he had more life to him, more vitality, than any man she'd ever known. But underlying these thoughts was the realization that she would be leaving in a few hours and in all probability would never see him again.

"Yes? What is it, Lauren?" he finally asked, his voice shattering the stillness.

She managed a smile. "If you'll buy me a drink, I'll give you the opportunity of experiencing something you've never experienced before."

He was nodding, almost smiling. "Yes, I remember. And I think I told you I had experienced everything."

"Have you, Early?"

He was smiling now. "I thought I had. I must admit you brought some novelty into my life. All three of you."

"I came to say goodbye."

"I know you did, Lauren. I thought I was going to avoid that. I suppose I thought that if I didn't appear at the farewell dinner, then maybe there wouldn't be a farewell."

"Don't make this more difficult for me than it already is."

His smile faded. "I'd like to make it so difficult that you won't leave." He was leaning back against the wardrobe now, his eyes on her clothes. "At least you didn't show up in your nightgown this time."

"I didn't want you to be able to accuse me of enticing you."

"The thing is, I find you just as enticing like that."

Lauren felt herself becoming warm. "Oh, Early, what are we going to do?"

"Come in the room, love, and close the door behind you." He spoke so softly, she had to listen to hear each word.

She moved into the room and closed the door quietly, then waited to see what would happen next.

He held out his arms. "Come here to me, Lauren."

Something held her back. "I don't think this is a good idea, Early."

"I think it's a very good idea."

She hesitated a moment, then realized he was right. It was a good idea, one she had thought about for so long it had created a permanent aching inside of her. Her need for him was so strong it had been keeping her awake nights with its intensity. She moved toward him slowly, almost flowing into his arms, and he pulled her close to him, not doing anything, just holding her.

"I want you so much, Lauren. Do you know, sometimes I think you were sent back in time just for me, because you're what I've always wanted and never met. Never could have met if this hadn't happened."

Lauren felt a smile forming and she looked up at him. "Oh, Early, don't start giving me some 'we were fated to meet' nonsense."

He scowled. "You know, you are the most unromantic female I've ever come across. If I want to think it was fate, then I'll think it was fate."

"Okay, Early, have it your way. I only hope you're still thinking of it as fate tomorrow and not the biggest mistake of your life."

"I have another theory."

Lauren sighed. All of them with their endless theories.

"This is the last theory, I promise you."

"Okay, let's hear it," she said, thinking the man was going to spend the rest of the night talking.

"I think if we were to make love, you'd never leave."

Lauren was relieved he was finally zeroing in on the subject at hand. "Want to test out that theory?"

"Yes, I want to test it out. But first I want to know what you think of it."

"I can give you a better assessment after the fact."

Early dropped his arms and stepped away from her. "I have a dire feeling that this is going to turn into one of those nights where we sit around arguing."

"Early, I don't want you to get your hopes up, that's all. I would very much like it if we spent our last night together making love, but I *will* leave in the morning."

He considered her words for a moment, then sat down on the side of his bed. "All right, we're not going to know either way until the deed is done, so come over here."

"The deed is done?" She was almost laughing.

"Get over here."

She walked over and stood in front of him. The bed was high, so they were at eye level. "It'll be interesting to see how they made love in the old days," she quipped.

"In the 'old days' the lady usually keeps quiet long enough for the gentleman to get on with it."

"I'm waiting. Make your best move."

Early leaned back on the bed with his elbows, shaking his head. "Damn it, Lauren, aren't you ever serious?"

"I'm a little nervous, that's all. I always joke around when I'm nervous."

"Maybe we *should* have a drink."

"Will you quit wasting time? We've only got all night."

He sat up again, this time putting his hands on the bottom of her sweat shirt and lifting it up. When it caught on her head, she helped him, pulling it off and then letting it fall to the floor. She looked at him, expecting to see desire in his eyes, but all she saw was curiosity.

"What is that *thing* you're wearing?"

"It's called a bra, Early. Just another tribute to modern technology."

"What does it do?"

Lauren glanced down. "In my case, not much. In a few years though, if it isn't worn out by then, it will no doubt hold me up."

He seemed to be searching for words, then finally said, "It's extremely sexy."

"Yeah, I can tell you're really getting carried away by it."

He smiled. "Still nervous?"

"Nervous verging on impatient."

"How does one remove it? I don't see any buttons."

"One removes it like this," she said, unfastening the front and allowing it to fall open. She was beginning to feel on display.

He was studying her with interest. "You're built differently from the women these days, I've noticed. So is Cindi."

"You mean we don't have that Gibson Girl shape?"

He nodded.

"Well, I'll tell you, Early, those women may look great with those hourglass figures when they're young, but give them a few years and they'll just look fat."

"I was only pointing out the difference. I quite like the way you look. And Cindi."

"Let's leave Cindi out of this, shall we?"

He collapsed back on the bed, convulsed with laughter. While he was enjoying the moment all by himself, she unzipped her jeans and kicked them off. She figured he was bent on taking so long with the preliminaries that she'd have to stay on a few days in San Francisco just to get to the finish.

He finally propped himself up on one elbow and looked at her. "Good lord, is that all you wear?"

"Pants and a bra, Early. It's quite sufficient."

"That's less than I wear."

"Well, I wouldn't know, would I? I haven't gotten to see you yet. And, Early, if you don't mind my saying so, you're taking all the romance out of this with your clinical observations. I know it's a first and all that—1906 man ravishes 1987 woman—but could we speed things up a little?"

"Let's not rush it, Lauren. This is a revelation to me. I've never had fun like this with a woman before. And don't give me that disbelieving look, because it's not sex I'm talking about."

Lauren decided to take the initiative. "You want to have fun, Early? Is that what you want?" She climbed up on the bed and crawled over to him. Reaching out, she began to unbutton his shirt while he watched her, his eyes filled with silent laughter. She tugged the bottom of the shirt out of his trousers, then pushed it back off his shoulders. "You're going to have to lift up a little, help me with this."

He propped himself up and let her take off his shirt, then she began to pull the undershirt over his head, thinking he'd come a long way since the day he wouldn't let her watch him put the sweatshirt on. She ran a hand over his smooth chest, then leaned over and kissed it. When she began to unbutton his pants she felt the stirring beneath, which told her that Early was capable of maintaining his sense of humor and getting an erection at the same time. That was good news, because for some reason she couldn't seem to get serious.

He lifted his hips so she could slide the pants down, then she was looking at the longest, baggiest set of underpants she'd ever seen. They were also scratchy to the touch. "How can you stand to wear those?" she asked.

"Don't stop now," said Early. "Get to the good part."

"Oh, you think you have a good part?"

He started to laugh, but then she did as he'd advised and found that he did indeed have a good part. A little shy to touch him, not knowing if that was done by respectable ladies these days, she instead lay down beside him and said, "Your move."

"Would you prefer I turned the lights out?"

"What for?"

"Just trying to protect your sensibilities, Lauren."

"I don't have any sensibilities."

He rolled toward her and pulled her bikini pants down over her hips, then she raised herself up while he removed them. She heard his indrawn breath. "You're even lovelier than I had pictured you in my mind."

"You mean you've been mentally undressing me, Early?"

"If you can't accept a compliment gracefully, Lauren, just keep that uncontrollable mouth of yours shut."

His head was moving toward hers and his eyes were closing when she said, "There's just one thing, Early."

The eyes opened. "What now?"

"I don't know how to say this without embarrassing you . . ."

"That's never stopped you before."

"You see, I was on the pill. Birth control pills, you wouldn't have heard of them. But they prevented me from getting pregnant. Anyway, I ran out of them a long time ago."

"Pills?"

"I don't feel like explaining them to you now, Early. If you're so interested you can ask Cindi later, she'll tell you. I just...if there's some way we could do it so I wouldn't be taking a chance...well, I'd appreciate it. I'm not saying I'm not going through with it in any case, though."

"This isn't the dark ages, Lauren. Of course I'll use protection."

"You mean you have something?"

He nodded. "And when the moment comes—if it ever *does* come—I'll put it on."

"Thank you, Early."

"You're welcome, Lauren."

This time when he bent over her she closed her eyes and wrapped her arms around him. As soon as they kissed she wondered why she had wasted so much time. This was better than arguing with Early, better than anything else with Early. She was a little surprised when his tongue entered her mouth; she hadn't been sure whether he did things like that. But so far he wasn't any different from a modern man, except he seemed to be putting a lot more feeling into it—and she found that she was, too.

When his lips finally moved down to caress her breasts, she ran her hands over his arms and his back, his skin smooth and warm to her touch. She was whispering, "Yes, oh, yes, Early, yes," and then his mouth moved farther down and she felt herself freeze. "What are you doing?" she asked, confused.

"Just relax, it's all right."

She lifted her head up to look at him. "I didn't think you'd do that."

"I won't if you keep talking," he said, and she let her head sink back, wondering what else he knew about that she hadn't thought he would.

It had been so long and she had wanted him so much that she felt herself almost instantly soaring, her hands clutching the bedspread as her head tossed back and forth. She tried to control herself, to go slowly, to savor the feeling, but her body surged out of her control, and she was crying out with the intensity of the feeling. Even as the small, diminishing shudders were still coming, like idle afterthoughts, she felt him lift himself up, and then he was reaching in the drawer of the bedstand and she wanted to watch, but she was still too paralyzed to move. Poised over her, his dark eyes clouded with desire, he kept repeating, "Lauren, Lauren," and then he entered her, and what she had thought was the ultimate before was compounded a hundredfold, and she was swept up and carried to heights that before had seemed insurmountable.

Later, as he rolled to her side and took her in his arms, his lips brushing her face, he said, "I knew it, I knew it would be like that."

Lauren sighed. "In its own way, that was every bit as devastating as the earthquake."

Early's body shook with silent laughter. "I couldn't *wait* to hear what you'd come out with. Comparing it to an earthquake, I should have guessed."

"That was supposed to be a compliment, Early." When he persisted in laughing, she added, "Actually, I'd rate it about an eight on the Richter scale."

His laughter quickly subsided. "The what?"

"It's the way earthquakes are measured—in my time, not yours," she replied smugly.

"Want to try for a twelve?"

She nestled her head against his shoulder. "Oh, Early, why have we wasted so much time?"

"It's been worth it. And we have the rest of our lives to work our way up the Richter scale. Tell me you'll stay, Lauren."

"No, I'm still leaving. But I think I may come back."

"Then come here," he said, his arms pulling her close. "Let me leave you with a few more reasons to hurry back."

Chapter Thirteen

**San Francisco Destroyed by Earthquake
Fire Surges Out of Control Through City**

SAN FRANCISCO, Apr. 18—A few seconds after 5:12 this morning, as thousands slept, an earthquake of jarring intensity struck the city. The deafening roar produced by the quake was matched only by the violence of the earth's movement as . . .

LAUREN AND KEVIN took the Union Southern Pacific railroad to Los Angeles. As Lauren remarked to Kevin after boarding the train, this was the first distinct improvement she had seen over 1987. The train was luxurious as well as immaculate, and any misgivings she had had about the trip subsided.

They arrived in Los Angeles late at night and hired a carriage, asking the driver to take them to a reasonably priced hotel.

Lauren looked out at the city but couldn't distinguish much in the dark. It was bound to seem different, though, even more different than San Francisco. Los Angeles had always been a city of cars to her, cars and freeways and gas stations on every corner, and drive-ins of all kinds, from eating places to movies to banks. Everything in L.A. was geared so that you never had to leave your car.

"You want to share a room, cut expenses?" Kevin asked her during the drive.

"I don't think so, Kevin. Anyway, these aren't the days of Holiday Inns with two queen-sized beds per room." What she didn't say was that she was exhausted. She hadn't slept at all the night before, and her plan to make up for it during the long train ride didn't work out—she'd been too nervous for sleep. Just knowing what was going to happen to Early in the next few hours was enough to make her jump at the slightest sound.

They checked into the hotel, paid in advance for the next two nights, then were shown to their rooms on the fifth floor. Lauren's was shabby with a sink in one corner that dripped water, but she didn't care. It had a bed and that was all she required at the moment.

She washed her face and hands in the sink and changed into one of her tie-dye outfits. A glance in the mirror told her she looked dreadful, but she thought some sleep would help. Once in bed, though, sleep wouldn't come. Maybe at this very moment the ground was moving under Early, and she had no way of knowing. He could be killed by a collapsing building or caught in a fire, and she might never learn what actually occurred. She didn't wish to be with him, though. If he was going to be killed she didn't want to see it, and as for herself, she was still convinced she wouldn't be able to psychologically survive two earthquakes, to say nothing of the fire. Early knew what he was getting into and could have left with them if he had wanted.

She tried to get her mind off Early by thinking of Cindi standing all alone in some corner of Fisherman's Wharf, waiting to be sent back to 1987. She didn't for a minute believe it would happen. She only hoped Cindi picked a spot where she wouldn't be hurt when the earthquake struck, but she gave her friend credit for enough sense to do so.

Finally she sat up and lit a cigarette, then got out of bed and pulled the cord for the overhead light. Moments later, there was a knock on the door and she heard Kevin say, "Need something to help you sleep?"

"How'd you know I was awake?" she asked, opening the door and letting him in.

"I was standing outside in the hall wondering if I should bother you when I saw the light go on. I couldn't sleep, either, so I bribed the night clerk to get me this." He held up a bottle of whiskey and Lauren smiled. "It didn't take us long to switch from mixed drinks with ice to straight whiskey, did it?"

"Actually," said Lauren, "that was about the easiest transition."

Kevin took a seat in the only chair and Lauren climbed back on the bed. They spent the next hour passing the bottle back and forth and wondering aloud what was happening in San Francisco.

"If we just had a TV," Kevin said at one point.

"I don't think I'd want to watch it. A radio, though . . ."

"Yeah. Something. Do you believe in the power of prayer?"

Lauren smiled. "No, but then I don't believe in time travel, either."

The last thing she remembered was closing her eyes and saying a little prayer for Early and Cindi, and then the sunlight streamed in through the window and woke her up. She glanced over to see Kevin, either asleep or passed out in the chair, then looked at her watch. It was eight o'clock. Something must have been heard from San Francisco by now.

She got dressed, then shook Kevin awake. "Come on, it's after eight. Let's go outside and see if anyone's heard anything."

He yawned and stretched, then went over to the sink and threw some cold water on his face. "I think I'm still drunk."

"Me too, a little. Maybe we can get some coffee downstairs and wake up."

Any doubts they might have had about the date they'd decided on were quickly dispelled as soon as they reached the lobby. It looked as though the quake had hit L.A. Through the open doors of the hotel, Lauren could see people running around and crowds gathering in the streets. A newsboy was standing in the center of the lobby, selling papers as fast as he could take people's money. Lauren pushed her way up to him, but by the time she got there they were all gone. She peered over someone's shoulder at the headline, nodded in resignation, then turned back to find Kevin.

"Did you see . . . ?" she asked him, and he nodded.

"At least Early was forewarned," he said. "He didn't just walk into it blind."

"I think it might be better not to know things in advance. It makes me feel...oh, somehow responsible, you know what I mean?"

"I know exactly what you mean, Lauren, but we weren't responsible and we did all we humanly could. You've just got to hang on to the thought that Early's all right. We're going to go get us some breakfast and make some plans. Okay?''

She nodded, trying to smile. "I'm so glad you're with me. Alone, I might have gone to pieces."

"You? No way, Lauren. You were the one who pulled us together, gave us all strength. Now come on, let's see that smile."

They left the hotel and Lauren stopped in surprise. "Look at this, Kevin—it looks like some of those towns you see in Westerns. Somehow I thought Los Angeles would be more like San Francisco."

"Except with palm trees."

"It's strange, isn't it? I think it might be harder to fit in here than it was up there."

"Maybe the city didn't boom until they started making movies here," he said, grabbing her arm and walking down the street. They found a place that served breakfast for 15 cents and had just given their order when Lauren announced, "I'm going back."

"I figured you would, but why don't you give it a few days first?"

"I can't. I've got to know now."

"Lauren, take it easy. Early will be all right. You know Early, he can take care of himself."

"Why did I leave?" she asked, her expression tormented.

"You know why you left. You'll be better for him now than if you'd had to live through another quake. Hey, what do you think happened to Cindi? You think right now she's at home, watching TV?"

Lauren was nodding. "Eating Mrs. Field's cookies. That's what she said she missed the most."

"God bless her. I hope she made it."

"I guess we'll never know."

"Hey, don't be so pessimistic. If she didn't go back, you'll hear from her again. Listen, you found her the first time, didn't you?"

"I wonder if I could telephone the *Chronicle* offices."

"Lauren, the quake *had* to disrupt all telephone lines. You might be able to telegraph up there, though."

"Are there telegraph offices, do you think?"

"I don't know, but we could find out."

"Let's try now, okay?"

Kevin took a good look at her, then nodded. "Sure. Hell, we can eat anytime."

"It seems so much different here," observed Lauren, once outside. "More so than San Francisco. I guess it's the absence of cars."

"And smog."

"You're right. Look, you can see the mountains."

Back at the hotel they asked the clerk where they could find a telegraph office and were given directions. On the way they bought a special edition of the *Times* and read it as they walked.

"They're not telling us anything we didn't already know," remarked Kevin.

"This is a really strange kind of déjà vu," said Lauren.

Kevin nodded. "You know, it'd make a weird movie—about these people who every time there's an earthquake get thrown back to 1906 and have to live through it all over again."

"Keep your creepy thoughts to yourself, Kevin."

"Come on, I was just trying to cheer you up."

"Well, if that's your idea of a cheering thought, locate your surfboard business in Long Beach. I think they get the next big quake."

The telegraph office was filled with people, and a clerk was announcing to the crowd that no messages could be sent to San Francisco by civilians, because the lines had to be kept open.

Los Angeles was taking on the air of a holiday. It didn't seem as though anyone went to work that day. When Kevin and Lauren walked back from the telegraph office, the streets were filled with people talking about the earthquake. There were already people on street corners collecting for the "Homeless San Franciscans," and everyone who walked by donated.

"I can't stand this," Lauren protested. "They're treating it like a carnival. Anything to get out of work, I guess."

"Don't be so hard on them," Kevin said. "They're upset about it, too. You're just feeling guilty 'cause you left."

"Yeah, I guess. Would you come to Union Station with me and see if I can get a ticket?"

"Why don't you wait a few days? You're going to arrive back in the middle of the fires."

"I'm not planning on walking right into them, Kevin. Give me credit for *some* sense."

The story was the same at Union Station. The ticket clerk queried, "San Francisco? You crazy, lady? Everyone else is trying to get *out* of the place, and you want to go there?"

"Please," said Lauren.

"Sorry, can't do it. The mayor up there wired for help, and all the trains are being commandeered for supplies going to Frisco."

Lauren turned helplessly to Kevin. "What am I going to do? Do I have to ride a horse up there?"

"Take it easy, Lauren."

"I feel so damn helpless! Why did I go so far? Why didn't I just go over to Oakland for the night?"

"'What ifs' aren't going to help right now, kid. Look, either Early's okay or he's not okay. Your going up there isn't going to change that. Listen, I've got an idea. Why don't we find some secluded beach, one where you can wear your bathing suit and I can wear my running shorts without getting arrested. Come on, you could stand to do a little relaxing."

"The *beach*? At a time like this?"

"You got any better ideas?"

It was several days before Lauren could get a train to San Francisco. Every day she went to Union Station and inquired, and every day she was turned away. Finally the ticket agent took pity on her and told her if she wanted to ride up there in a supply car, that was her decision. It was fine with Lauren; by that time she was ready to walk.

Kevin took her to the station, and one last time she begged him, "Come back with me, Kevin."

"We've been over this before, Lauren."

"But it doesn't make any sense. The surfboards were my idea, not yours. I figured you were only humoring me."

"It has nothing to do with that."

"Then why? At least you know people in San Francisco. We survivors have to stick together, Kevin."

"That's just why I'm not coming with you."

"I really don't understand that."

"It's simple, Lauren. As long as we stick together we're always going to be the survivors from 1987. I think the sooner I get with people who don't know about that, the sooner I'm going to begin to forget and start living again. Being with you, being with someone from my own time…well, it just reminds me of my wife, that's all. It's time to forget all that. We're stuck here for good and no wishful thinking is going to make it otherwise."

"I don't agree, Kevin. It's like living in a foreign country. You find other Americans so you have someone to talk to, someone you have something in common with."

"That's not the way I see it. When you do that, then you're always an expatriate, you never really belong. As long as I'm stuck here for sure, I want to belong. Otherwise, if I don't make that effort, what I lost is just going to eat away at me and I won't be any good for anything."

Lauren put her arms around him and rested her face against his chest. "I'm glad we got to know each other, anyway. I'll be reading the papers, Kevin, expecting to see you in them one of these days as the champion surfer."

"Hell, the *only* surfer. And listen, Lauren, I hope you find Early okay. When you do, give my regards to him. He's a good man. None better."

THE CITY was a shambles.

There was no public transportation in evidence and Lauren walked slowly from the train station, trying to regain her bearings. Rain had come during the night to settle the ash, and the air was clear except for silvery white traces of steam rising from the damp, hot ruins. Thousands of acres of quiet desolation remained where for days one of the worst fires in history had raged.

Only scattered fragments of the city remained. She had read accounts in the newspapers that the new City Hall and all its records, the libraries, the courts and jails, the theaters and restaurants had all vanished. Thirty schools, eighty churches and convents, the business sections and the homes of 250,000 San Franciscans had been destroyed. There was little in the way of food and goods, no transportation or communication system, and in the latest toll more than 450 were dead.

As she walked she wondered where all the people were. She saw a sign posted on the side of a wall, the only remaining part of what previously had been a building.

Proclamation

by the Mayor

The Federal Troops, the members of the Regular Police Force and all Special Police Officers have been authorized by me to KILL any and all persons found engaged in Looting or in the Commission of Any Other Crime. I have directed all the Gas and Electric Lighting Co.'s not to turn on Gas or Electricity until I order them to do so. You may therefore expect the city to remain in darkness for an indefinite time. I request all citizens to remain at home from darkness until daylight every night until order is restored. I WARN all Citizens of the danger of fire from Damaged or Destroyed Chimneys, Broken or Leaking Gas Pipes or Fixtures, or any like cause.

                                        E. E. Schmitz, Mayor

Gradually, she began to gain a sense of location. She made her way downtown to the area where the Chronicle Building had been, but it was gone, as she knew it would be. She had heard that all the San Francisco newspapers were now operating out of a similar facility in Oakland, but she didn't have any idea how to get to Oakland. Anyway, the story was in San Francisco, not Oakland; surely the reporters would be here.

She had thought for a time it had been a mistake to leave; now she was convinced it was a bigger mistake to have returned. This was worse, far worse, than being thrown back in time. She had survived that, but she didn't know what to do now. She was one more person among thousands of homeless, and she didn't know where to turn.

She kept walking, hoping to find somewhere to stay before dark. The supplies they had left for Early had been in vain, because when she found his neighborhood, only sections of two small structures remained. Early's house had vanished.

With no hope of finding him, she headed in the direction of Chinatown. If Cindi was still around, she thought that was where she would have headed. When she got to the area Chinatown had occupied, there was nothing but rubble. The scene exactly resembled pictures she had seen of places that had been bombed during wars. She caught sight of a piece of paper fluttering in the wind, drifting in the ruins, and she reached down and picked it up. It said:

Warning

Notice is Given that any person found Pilfering, Stealing, Robbing, or committing any act of Lawless Violence will be summarily HANGED.

Vigilance Committee

She held on to her duffle bag more tightly. In Los Angeles she had made the final gesture and thrown out all the clothes and useless possessions from her former life. Instead, she had filled the bag with as many sandwiches, bottles of whiskey and soft drinks that she could squeeze in, plus cigarettes and candy for energy and even a few candles. It was now a survival kit, and she didn't want to lose it.

She had also changed into her jeans, sweatshirt and leather jacket, but not because she couldn't part with them. They were the most practical clothes for riding in a stock car full of provisions and for the camping out she might have to do. In the midst of a disaster, no one was going to be worried about what anyone else was wearing. She was sure that most of the survivors had grabbed the first clothes that came to hand and run for their lives.

When she finally saw someone it was a policeman who appeared to be standing guard at one of the street corners. "I just got to town," she said to him. "I'm looking for my husband."

He tipped his hat, not even giving her clothes a glance. "Can I be of any help to you, ma'am?"

"Where is everyone? The survivors?"

"Well, they're mostly scattered. A lot of them are camping out in Golden State Park, but the majority's over to Oakland."

"How do I get to Oakland?"

"I suggest you go down to the waterfront, try to get across on one of the ferryboats. The newspapers are all running out of Oakland now. They're listing names of missing people. Perhaps you could put your husband's name in there."

SHE WAS ABLE to exchange a bottle of whiskey for a boat ride to Oakland and thought it cheap at the price. When the man had refused to take her and she'd offered him the whiskey, he said, "Lady, for a bottle of whiskey I'll take you *anywhere*," and the bargain had been struck.

She had never seen 1906 Oakland. As a matter of fact, she had seen 1987 Oakland only once, when she had to fly out of its airport, so she didn't know how much it had changed. Except for slight damage to one building she passed, the city didn't appear to have suffered from the quake.

She asked everyone she passed if they knew where the *San Francisco Chronicle* was publishing from, but no one seemed to know. Finally, when it began to get dark, she asked if anyone knew where the relocation camps were, and was told of several. One, she learned, was for the refugees from Chinatown, and with the hope of finding Cindi, she headed in that direction.

When she arrived, the probability of finding anyone seemed nil. The area was as crowded as an outdoor rock concert. She walked among the people, but everyone was dressed in black and she had trouble distinguishing features in the fading light. When it was too dark and she was too tired to go on, she found a spot beneath a tree and sat down on the ground, prepared to spend the night there and search for Cindi again in the morning.

Some people had small fires going and were cooking what little food they had. She unwrapped one of the sandwiches but only ate half. She didn't know where or when she'd get more food after her supply ran out. A couple of shots of whiskey helped put her to sleep, but with the first light in the sky she was up and looking for Cindi again.

As she walked she called Cindi's name, scanning faces for her familiar smile. And then, in the distance, she saw her. If it hadn't been for the tie-dyed outfit Cindi was wearing, Lauren didn't think she would have found her.

She made her way slowly through the crowds of people, who entirely covered the surface of the ground. When she got within a few feet, she called, "Cindi!"

Cindi turned and saw her, and then they were moving toward each other as quickly as they could manage. Hugging her friend to her at last, Lauren cried, "Oh, God—I think I'm even happier to find you this time than the first. What a terrible nightmare this is."

"Did you see Chinatown?"

"There was nothing left of it."

"They moved them all here, Lauren, but nothing's being done for them. I'm trying to organize the children, keep them occupied so their parents can try to find food. But there are so many of them it seems hopeless."

"What happened, Cindi? Did you go to Fisherman's Wharf as you planned?"

Cindi nodded. "Fool that I was."

"Don't say that. It was worth the try."

"I guess miracles don't occur when you're standing waiting for them. Is Kevin with you?"

"He stayed in Los Angeles."

"I knew you'd be back. Have you been able to find Early?"

She shook her head. "I hear the newspaper people are all over here, but I can't find out where."

"You'll find him, I know you will. If ever two people were meant to end up together..."

Children were coming up to Cindi and staring up at her, tugging at her pants. Lauren asked, "What can I do to help?"

"You mean it?"

"Of course I mean it."

"The biggest thing right now is getting some water for them. You wouldn't believe how they're treated, Lauren, like they aren't even human. And they're too shy to ask for anything. It makes me cry. They had so little before and now they have nothing. You should have heard me with some of the officials who came around. I think it's the first time they've ever been talked back to by a Chinese. And I think you'd be a real help, *not* being Chinese."

"We'll make sure something's done for them," Lauren assured her. "You and I know a little about demonstrations, if nothing else. And those notices we printed up? We'll flood this city with notices on how the Chinese are being treated. There must be some people who care."

"It's great," said Cindi. "I think together we can get something accomplished. But find Early first, Lauren. Set your mind at rest and then come back and help. I don't think it'll take you that long—ask one of the cops, they should know."

Lauren set her dufflebag down on the ground. "Can I leave this here? There's some food and drinks inside, and some candy you could give the children. Do whatever you think best with it."

"You want to hear something, Lauren?"

"Sure."

"I have this new theory—now don't laugh—I think I was sent back here for this. To help them."

Lauren shook her head, resigned. "Early thinks I was sent back for him, you think you were sent back to help the Chinese earthquake victims.... I don't know, maybe you're right and I'm wrong because I can't make any sense of it. Maybe I was sent back because I was enjoying my life then too much."

"Go on—act cynical. But I know you better."

WHEN SHE FINALLY FOUND the building the *Chronicle* was using, Lauren didn't find Early, but Henry Hawkins was very much in evidence.

"Lauren," he shouted over the noise, "I heard you moved to Los Angeles."

She accepted his hug. "Would I desert you, H.H.?"

"Early said—"

"Is he all right?"

"Early? Of course he's all right. You mean you haven't seen him?"

"I just got back last night."

"Well, he's fine. As good as can be expected. Take a seat over there, Lauren, he should be back soon."

"Could I leave a note for him instead?"

"Help yourself. Give it to me and I'll be sure he gets it. But don't disappear on me again, Lauren. We'll be back in business soon, and more people than ever are going to need that good advice of yours."

Good advice? She could hardly believe what she was hearing. Could the earthquake have mellowed H.H. to that extent?

FEELINGS AGAINST the Chinese seemed to run as strong in Oakland as in San Francisco, and for a while, as Lauren and Cindi scoured the neighborhoods begging for help, they felt as if they were beating their heads against a wall.

But then, in a poorer section of town where they began to see more blacks than whites, they spotted a church, and Lauren said, "Come on, Cindi, let's remind them of Christian charity."

Lauren was ashamed of her race when she found the only help forthcoming was from the preacher of the Baptist church. She and Cindi had walked into the church during an evening service of some kind, and instead of being thrown out, as they had anticipated, the preacher gazed down at them from the pulpit and, very politely, asked what they wanted.

Lauren took a deep breath, suddenly nervous with all eyes on her. "It's the Chinese in the relocation camp, sir.

No one will help them. They're out of water and food and they don't even have any blankets. If you could spare *anything*..."

The preacher looked down at his congregation. "Well, you heard the lady. What are you folks waiting for?"

It wasn't more than a half hour before the church members returned, each carrying something to donate to the refugees. Then, led by Cindi and Lauren and the preacher, they paraded down the street in the direction of the camp.

"This is so good of you," Cindi told the preacher at one point.

"We know what it's like to feel unwanted, child."

"Well, we thank you, and I want you to know you've made some friends. They won't forget your kindness."

And so, for that night at least, most of the Chinese refugees had a little something to eat, a ration of water, and the children were put to sleep under the blankets. Tomorrow she and Cindi would think of other ways to help them.

"I thought Early would be here by now," said Cindi, once they had finished their work for the evening.

"He wouldn't find us in the dark. Anyway, we don't need to worry about Early. He's okay and he knows where we are. I wonder if things will ever get back to normal?"

"I don't think for a long time. But we know the city is eventually rebuilt. You know what I'm going to do, Lauren?"

"Design clothes."

"No, clothes aren't important. Fun maybe, but not really important. I'm going to start a school for those children. You know they don't go to public schools because they can't speak English? I figure I can at least teach them English, give them a chance. I honestly think I could be of some help to them.''

"You'll give them hope, anyway. And I think we could get Early to do some articles on the Chinese, what they have to go through. Not right away, though. I imagine for quite a while the only news is going to be about the earthquake. Where do you suppose all these people are going to live?''

"They're putting up tents in places,'' Cindi told her, "whole cities of tents.''

"Maybe we should have made tents instead of lounging pajamas from Paris. We could've made a fortune.''

"I don't feel like that anymore, Lauren. It's funny, but I feel I belong now. I went through this just like they did, and now I'm where I belong.''

"I feel like that too, Cindi,'' said Lauren. "I don't even mind so much being back here, anymore.''

"And of course there's Early.''

"Yes,'' said Lauren, "that, too.''

Aftermath

IT WAS ALMOST NOON when Early arrived.

Cindi and Lauren had been up since dawn rationing out the remaining supplies of water and food from the night before. There was enough to sustain the people for a few more hours, but they had work to do, more provisions to find. At about eight in the morning the preacher, whom they now learned was Reverend George Colter, arrived at the campsite with two horse-drawn wagons filled to capacity with gallon jugs of water and a plentiful supply of canned goods.

"Benefit of the ladies' prayer group," he had told them, and Lauren had said, "Oh, how I wish we could pay you for all this."

"We'll be repaid," he told her.

After that they set up a food center in the camp, and as word got out, a seemingly endless line of refugees formed. The people, silent, heads bowed, stood for hours as Cindi and Lauren portioned out rations of water and food.

Lauren was filling a cup with water for one of the children in line when Early appeared. She saw him at once, since he towered over everyone else, and he stood for a moment watching her in silence.

Then he took her hand. "Cindi can handle things for a minute," he told her. "Come, let me see you."

They walked a short distance away and stood, simply gazing at each other, until Early broke the silence again. "Look at you, you're as dark as me." His hand went out to caress her cheek, push her hair back out of her eyes. "With those dark eyes and that dark skin, you could be as Spanish as I am. What have you been doing down there in Southern California to get that dark?"

"Oh, Early," she said, throwing herself against him and holding him with all her strength. "I'm so sorry I left. I don't know why I didn't stay with you."

"No, Lauren, don't have any regrets. I was glad you weren't here. If you had been, half my worries would have been for your safety. And you're back now."

"I'll never leave again, Early, I promise you."

He took hold of her arms and held her away from him as he looked into her eyes. "Now don't go making any rash promises you might not be able to keep. Who knows, maybe some time machine will be invented one of these days and you'll want to go back."

She was shaking her head. "I don't want to go back, anymore. I realized that in Los Angeles."

"You mean you're content to stay here with a man old enough to be your grandfather?"

She started to say something, then changed her mind. Stepping back from him, she said, "Why is it, Early, that when for the first time I try to inject some romance into our relationship, when I'm all prepared for a touching reunion, *you* have to start in on *that* again?"

Early stood there and laughed, the sound of it joyful to her ears. "Because it's going to be rough, Lauren. Because we're not going to be able to walk into the sunset and live happily ever after. There's a lot of hard work ahead of us, as you can see for yourself here. And because I want the old Lauren back again, not this new romantic version you're trying to foist off on me.''

"Well, all right," she said, still a little miffed.

"Come here, woman, let me kiss you."

"In public, Early? With people watching?"

"Well hell, Lauren, I figure we can meet halfway in those conventions of ours."

He moved to her and took her in his arms, and as his mouth pressed hungrily against hers, she knew that the only place she wanted to be, and the only time she wanted to be in, were here and now—with Early.

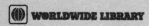